THE MORTSAFE

Other titles by Lillian Stewart Carl:

The *Sabazel* series:

Sabazel
The Winter King
Shadow Dancers
Wings of Power

The *Ashes to Ashes* series:

Ashes to Ashes
Dust to Dust
Garden of Thorns

The Jean Fairbairn/Alasdair Cameron series:

The Secret Portrait
The Murder Hole
The Burning Glass
The Charm Stone
The Blue Hackle

Stand-alone novels:

Memory and Desire
Shadows in Scarlet
Time Enough to Die
Lucifer's Crown
Blackness Tower

Short Story collections:

Along the Rim of Time
The Muse and Other Stories of History, Mystery, and Myth

Non-fiction:

The Vorkosigan Companion (with John Helfers)

THE MORTSAFE

A Short Jean Fairbairn/Alasdair Cameron Mystery
Book Six in the Series

Lillian Stewart Carl

ACKNOWLEDGEMENTS

This is an original, never-before-published novel.

DEDICATION

For Garda, founding mother of the muses.

Chapter One

Jean Fairbairn handed her section of *The Scotsman* across the table, then snatched it back, just missing the teapot and the toast rack. "Whoa," she said.

Alasdair Cameron didn't look up from his own carefully folded page. "Eh?"

"Wow!" She angled the newsprint toward the lamp, since precious little light was leaking through the window this drippy, dreary—dreich, in Scotspeak—Edinburgh dawn.

"Aye?"

Jean peered over the edge of the paper, and over the rings on her left hand holding the paper, at her husband. Her new, improved, husband. Who'd have guessed that her first marriage would turn out to be a twenty-year-long beta test? What his first marriage had been . . . Well, no point in going there, not again.

"Alasdair, we haven't been married long enough to talk to each other in monosyllables."

"Right." His keen blue eyes sparked above the rims of his reading glasses. "I might as well be asking what you've found in yon paper, then, as you'll be telling me about it anyway."

"Come on. You're as curious as a cat."

Removing his glasses, he turned his gaze toward the gray fur lump on the window seat that was Dougie. The sleeping cat looked like a frayed sweater, carelessly abandoned. Alasdair swiveled back to Jean, one brow cocked in his best Mr. Spock impersonation.

Since Jean had read in a psychology magazine that rolling your eyes at your significant other meant problems in a relationship, she focused steadily on a small block of type at the bottom of the page beneath the transcript of some arcane political discussion in the Scottish Parliament. Parliamentary fog no doubt explained the weeks of cloud and drizzle, just as the hot air emanating from the Texas Legislature, back on her native turf, explained summer heat waves.

"Protect and Survive has a contract with the owner of that new pub on the South Bridge, doesn't it? You know, the one going into the old Playfair Building, across the street from Lady Niddry's House?"

"We've got contracts with half the businesses in that area, not to mention the university. I don't doubt the pub's one of them, aye. Why? Did they have a break-in?"

It had taken her an entire year to get it into her head that "I doubt" sometimes meant "I suspect", and then he threw the usual meaning at her. "They had more of a break-out. A couple of plumbers were doing their thing in the cellar and part of the wall collapsed into one of the vaults beneath the street."

"There's—what? Eighteen vaults? Nineteen? And only the arch over the lower street, the Cowgate, not invisible."

"In the strict sense of invisible, yes, in that with all the buildings along the top of the bridge and down the sides there's only one place you can tell that the South Bridge street is really that, a bridge. But vaults don't swim in and out of the space-time continuum."

Crinkles were forming at the corners of his eyes, complementing the one at the corner of his mouth and making him look more like a low-key Captain Kirk than Mr. Spock. "Depends on who you're asking, eh?"

"Well, yeah. It does. Anyway, the plumbers, being a heckuva lot braver souls than I am, climbed through the gap in the wall and found a chamber containing two dead bodies. Although in this context, 'bodies' would imply dead."

"How dead?" The crinkles went lopsided. He reached for the page with his left hand, its plain gold band glinting in the lamplight, and with his right hand replaced his glasses.

Jean handed the page over. "It doesn't say, but I doubt—I don't think—they're recent. Not that the environment of the vaults and how it affects human decay is anything I want to consider over breakfast." She spread the last piece of toast thickly with butter—when in Scotland, butterfat wasn't calories, it was insulation—and heaped on strawberry jam.

Alasdair said, half to himself, "The bodies were found late yesterday afternoon and Lothian and Borders Police is investigating. They'll not yet have removed them, I reckon . . ."

The electronic melody of "Hail to the Chief" interrupted him. Abandoning her toast, Jean went to find first her mini–backpack and brain storage unit, and then, inside it, her phone.

From the second floor of the apartment came the double bleat of Alasdair's ring tone. Abandoning the newspaper, he headed off toward the room that Jean called his man-cave but that he, dignity affronted, referred to as his study. A good thing they'd bought the flat next door to the one where she'd been living alone. Two tiny apartments combined into a small-to-medium one equaled enough space they could live together, independent but contiguous entities.

Jean switched on the phone and pressed it to her ear. "Good morning, Miranda."

"Good morning to you." This time of day Miranda's voice was smoky from Lapsang Souchong tea served in fine china, not from single-malt served in cut glass. "You've seen the paper, then?"

Miranda's ESP, Jean thought for the hundredth time, was much more useful than her and Alasdair's ghost-activated sixth senses. "The article about the workmen breaking into the vault beneath the new pub? Oh yeah, I've seen it."

"No flies on you, Jean. Got it in one. Are you thinking what I'm thinking?"

"Of course I am. Since it all seems to be more historical than contemporary, it might in due course make a fine article for *Great Scot*. Just as long as I don't have to spend too much time blundering around in the South Bridge vaults."

"Ah, the tourist companies have those vaults mapped out like interchanges on the M6. Lights, cameras, action, the lot. No need for your claustrophobia to go acting up."

"And how about my . . ." She wasn't going to use the word fear, even to one of her best friends, and her only employer and business partner. ". . . lack of interest in blundering around in the dark? There's many a story of tour groups getting down into those vaults and the lights going off."

"And ghosties and ghoulies pinching and scratching. Oh aye." Paper rustled and china rang.

Jean strolled back to the table and refilled her mug. "This part of Edinburgh's teeming with so many ghost stories the poor souls would have to take numbers and wait their turn before saying boo. The Castle, the Vaults, Mary King's Close, Greyfriars Kirkyard across from the Museum."

"Are there that many poor souls still out and about, Jean?"

"A few, yes, but they're outnumbered by the story-mongers and the gullible. And there are none right here in Ramsay Garden, let me hasten to add, any more than there are in the office."

"Makes no matter to me. I'm not sensitive. Few to none of the tourists are, either, but there's no need for such tales to be true to come a treat to them. A good shiver and a nice wee dram afterwards, part of the Scottish experience. The owner of the new pub likely ordered the tradesmen to ca' down the wall, the better to increase his trade. He's named the place The Resurrectionist Bar."

"The Resurrectionist?"

"Not the best name, from a marketing standpoint."

"Well, it's a bit more elegant than Body Snatchers Are Us." Jean laughed, if wryly. How many of Scotland's darkest moments, even body snatchers or resurrection men like Burke and Hare, were now no more than scenic overlooks along the historical trail?

Through the arched opening between her old living room—now the dining room—and the new one echoed Alasdair's voice: "The city's honeycombed with forgotten passages and cellars. Dozens of bodies are likely moldering away in obscure corners. If I was owner of The Resurrectionist, I'd be more concerned about living bodies breaking, entering, vandalizing—the lot."

Ah, so someone *had* contacted Protect and Survive, the

agency specializing in security for historic properties that Alasdair was now heading up. Was the owner concerned about concealed postern gates below his property? Or did Lothian and Borders, the local cop shop, want ex-cop Alasdair's opinion on the convergence of history and—well, no one had suggested any crimes, not yet.

"We'll see how wedded Vasudev is to The Resurrectionist when we're interviewing him the day," Miranda was saying. "He might be taking suggestions, still."

"Who?"

"Vasudev Prasad. He's by way of owning the property, though my own Duncan holds a high enough percentage that Vasudev was quite obliging when I rang him up and suggested he call at the office soon as may be."

"No flies on you, either, Miranda. Barely nine in the morning and you're hard at work."

"As am I." Alasdair walked back into the dining room, carrying not his cell phone but his toothbrush. "Herself is sending you to the scene, is she? You might as well have a wee dauner down that way with me, then. I've been called out as well, Lothian and Borders rang Ian at the office, saying a D.I. Knox wants a word."

"There's a good Edinburgh name, Knox. Any relation to the sixteenth-century theological gadfly, I wonder?" Jean turned back to her phone. "Miranda . . ."

"Well done," Miranda told her. "You and Alasdair can be interviewing the police as a team, see what sort of mystery's been brought to the light of day, eh?"

"Or whether there's any mystery at all," Jean replied, well accustomed to playing the damp blanket to Miranda's commercial exuberance. "The bodies are probably those of some poor—literally poor, as in low or no-income—people who didn't have anywhere else to live, or die, for that matter, and when the vaults were walled up so were their bodies."

"Oooh. There you are. What's that story by Edgar Allan Poe about the jester bricked up in the wall? 'A Cask of Amontillado?' A grand sherry, Amontillado."

"So would this be 'A Cask of Single Malt?'"

"If you're turning up a whisky-distilling angle, better and better. I'll have a look amongst our advertisers, see who was in business—when were the vaults closed up?"

Jean quelled her laugh. She had to stop teasing Miranda—it was like shooting fish in a barrel. Although why you would want to shoot fish in a barrel, she had no idea. "Late 1800s, depending . . ."

Using the heel of the toothbrush to point to his watch, Alasdair called loudly, "Later, Miranda."

"I'll be waiting at the office, Jean," Miranda said, "with bated breath and hot coffee. Cheerie-bye."

"Bye-bye." Jean switched off the phone, inhaled the last bite of toast—even preserved in thick syrup, the strawberries hinted of summer fields warmed by sunshine—and washed it down with tea.

Chapter Two

Within moments, she and Alasdair had shoveled the dishes into the dishwasher, made themselves both presentable and weatherproof, and set out into the mizzle. The flowerpots beside the porch held no spring tulips for them to tiptoe through, but they did tread quietly past the flat next door. Since its curtains were still tightly drawn, musician Hugh Munro was no doubt sleeping off a late-night gig.

Ramsay Garden was set just below a corner of the castle esplanade, the parade ground before the castle gates. Next to the grim medieval fortress, the whimsical, whitewashed, turn-of-the-last-century buildings looked like a parade of garden gnomes. Since the first rule of real estate was location, location, location, the apartments were both desirable and expensive. They were also noisy, especially when multitudes of tourists and battalions of marching bands occupied the esplanade during the summer months.

Jean peered through the moisture gathering on her glasses, tugged the hood of her coat further over her brow, and told herself there was one reason to like winter. It was quiet. Dark, wet, and cold, but quiet—if with the ongoing soundtrack from Hugh. A good thing he and his band played traditional-style music rather than heavy metal or jazz.

She stepped out both briskly and carefully, the first to keep up with Alasdair's stride across the courtyard, the second to avoid a pratfall on the steep flank of Ramsay Lane with its picturesque but slippery cobblestones. When he offered her his arm, she grasped it. Standing on feminist principles worked better if she was standing, period.

At the High Street they turned away from the looming pile of the castle and headed east, down the fissure between tall medieval buildings that visitors knew as the Royal Mile. This time of year the tartanalia shops behind their contemporary ground floor facades claimed less territory, racks of polyester plaid, postcards, plastic swords and Loch Ness monsters stored inside. Above them dark, mossy stone walls rose like cliffs toward the gray sky. Only the occasional bright red hearts-and-flowers Valentine's Day window display mitigated the gloom.

Jean glanced across at St. Giles Cathedral, large but only relatively stern with its decorative crown of a spire, today more damp than devout. "I hope John Knox's grave is large enough for him spin efficiently—especially since it's now beneath the car park."

"There's one historical figure," Alasdair returned, "not rumored to be haunting."

"He's not glamorous enough. Not like the Catholic queens he loathed. I mean, it clearly says in the Bible that weak sissy females aren't suppose to rule men, right?"

"And yet he favored democracy and universal education, if not by today's definitions."

"Another of Edinburgh's Jekyll and Hyde figures." Dodging an umbrella—fortunately she was so short an out-of-control rib was hardly likely to jab her in the eye—Jean considered the windows of the cafés and coffee bars. They were so smudged with steam the customers inside look like sea creatures under water.

The warmth of her breakfast was fading, and the chill breeze oozing up the street scoured her cheeks and nose. By the time they reached their destination her complexion, a shade of pale she thought of as belly-of-newt, would be pink and raw. She inhaled the aroma of hot bread, frying bacon, and, above all, coffee, the elixir of life. She might drink tea with Alasdair over breakfast, but that was only to sustain her long enough to get to the *Great Scot* coffee maker.

Alasdair gently but firmly pulled her back onto the straight and narrow of the sidewalk. "When I was at university," he said, "I'd stop by a café on Argyle Street and have myself a bacon, egg, and bean pie for ninety-nine p. Made a grand breakfast."

"Bacon, eggs, and beans in a crust? Only the British stomach could tolerate that."

"Not so different from one of your breakfast burritos, I'm thinking, and here's your lot adding hot peppers to boot." His shudder was no doubt amplified for effect.

"Right," she told him, and went on, "Were the winters this cold and dark in Glasgow?"

"Oh aye. Seems worse here, though, with the buildings frowning down like Knox himself."

"John? Or D.I? Some of these detectives can be pretty harsh."

"To go using your own words: You think?" Alasdair's laugh was considerably drier than the air. "I've never met this chap. No need to go jumping to conclusions, never mind that's your favorite exercise."

"You think?" she returned with a grin.

Together they crossed the street and rounded the flank of the Tron Kirk, no longer a religious establishment but a museum. There they paused, at the junction not just of two streets but of two eras, gazing south down a busy avenue lined with foursquare classical facades. After over two hundred years of Edinburgh weather, the buildings of the South Bridge appeared as dark and inscrutable as those on the High Street, never mind the occasional pediment or porch and the dome of the old college rising in the distance.

For centuries the population of the city had huddled along the ridge running down from the castle, behind stone walls, building taller and taller tenements on either side of what was now the High Street. Jean hated to think what the place had smelled like. Even people of the time, whose noses had to have been considerably less delicate than modern ones, had complained.

Then, by the 1780s, not only all the local British wars but that pesky American Revolution had passed. England was so firmly in control that Scotland was just 'North Britain'—which at least gave Edinburghians the chance to spill out of the old city, bridging the valleys to the north and south of the High

Street with vaulted roads similar to viaducts.

Soon buildings lined the street atop the South Bridge, and more clambered down its sides, almost filling in the valley and leaving only the narrow street of the Cowgate, which passed far below the Bridge through its one exposed arch. The hidden arches supporting the bridge, the vaults, were originally used for storage, small shops, and work areas. But they were wet, lacked ventilation, and became slums where the poor had huddled hopelessly.

"The South Bridge vaults were evacuated and sealed off at the end of the nineteenth century?" Alasdair asked, always sure to double-check his sources.

"Yep" replied Jean. "They were—well, 'rediscovered' isn't the right word—re-opened in the 1990s."

"And now there are so many pubs and nightclubs both above and belowstairs, I'm thinking most of the spirits reported are less paranormal than high-proof. Shall we?"

Chuckling, Jean once again fell into step beside him.

"Opposite Lady Niddry's House, Ian was saying. Not so far along the street as the arch over the Cowgate, where there were buildings lost during the 2002 fire, but near. And wasn't that a headache for the firefighters, tracking the fire into the catacombs."

Jean could imagine, but didn't. "You know that Lady Niddry's House is just another marketing scheme, don't you? There never was a Lady Niddry, just an alley, Niddry's Wynd, running down from the High Street to the Cowgate and covered over by the bridge."

"Nothing like a hint of the aristocracy, I'm thinking, for posh shops and a restaurant."

"As posh as you're going to get in this neighborhood, anyway."

Jean skirted a puddle, and a thin stream of water pouring off an overhang, and checked out the funky outliers of the university: shops selling casual clothing, comic books, music and videos, computer and electronic gear, food and drink. Flags hung dispiritedly from the front of a hotel. Backpack-wearing students clambered off buses, slammed in and out of various doorways, stopped at ATMs. And, a block down the street, a police car with all its lights flashing came to a sudden halt.

"That's across from Lady Niddry's House." Jean quickened her pace.

But her journalist instincts didn't perk up any faster than Alasdair's police whiskers. He was already moving, half a pace ahead of her.

A constable leaped out of the car and ran into a classical Age-of-Reason structure whose ground floor had been carried by time and taste into the Age of Commerce. Passers-by began to coagulate around the door.

Alasdair reached around, and without even looking grabbed Jean's forearm—the magnetic attraction of wedding ring to wedding ring, she supposed—and pulled her behind him through the bodies and their miasma of wet wool sweaters. Electronic voices crackled from the squad car, overridden by the sub-vocal buzz of the kibitzers.

Of the building, Jean noticed only a plate glass window blocked with brown paper and a wooden door covered in peeling paint, ajar behind a sheet of water falling from somewhere overhead. Then Alasdair thrust the door open and they were through the icy waterfall and inside.

Blinking through her water-flecked glasses, she saw that they were in a dark, chilly hallway piled with construction material. With one hand she groped in her pocket for a tissue and with the other she swept the hood off her head. A woman's shrill voice echoed in the gloom. "It's my sister. I know it's my sister. Let me in. Let me see her."

A man's voice murmured, "Now miss—nothing definite— no need to worry yourself . . ."

Jean mopped at her glasses and jammed them back onto her face just as a constable surged forward, made a warding gesture, and inhaled to speak. Alasdair spoke first. "Alasdair Cameron from Protect and Survive. Jean Fairbairn. D.I. Knox is expecting us."

"Down you go, then," the constable returned, with a quick

sidestep and a gesture behind him. "Have a care for the red-headed hellion."

"Ta." Alasdair headed on down the hall, past the doors leading into a large room filled with a long counter, mirrors, lamps, tables, now all dark and disarranged but soon to be, no doubt, The Resurrectionist Bar. A flight of stairs ran upward into shadow. The light coming from below them no doubt emanated from the cellar door.

Was it Tolkien, Jean wondered, who'd once said "cellar door" were the prettiest words in the language, if you considered only their sound and not their meaning? But Jean was considering their meaning.

Behind her back, the constable blocked the street door and murmured some variation on, "Move along, nothing to see here."

From the open doorway, the first voice shrilled, "You dinna understand, 'twas just here she went missing, fifteen years since, I know it's her . . ."

Another female voice, this one an acidic contralto, said, "Either calm yourself or I'll have you removed from the premises."

Alasdair made a hard left into the throat of the stairwell, redolent with the chemical scent of paint, then looked back over his shoulder. His hair caught the glow of a bare bulb, the silver threads and the gold alike emitting a subtle gleam. "Jean?"

"I'm okay. I'm coming." She pushed away any deliberations on cellars in general and the South Bridge vaults in particular.

"Well done." He creaked on down the narrow steps to a landing, Jean so close behind him the hem of his coat flew back into her legs . . . An upwards rush and a woman catapulted into Alasdair's chest. He didn't so much leap as fall backwards, smashing Jean in turn against the wall.

"Here!" shouted a male voice from below, and, in chorus, a light female voice called, "Stop just there!"

Swiftly regaining his balance, Alasdair seized the woman

with both hands and held her in front of him like a veterinarian holding a clawing kitten. "You're all right then," he said, not to her but from the corner of his mouth to Jean.

"Yeah. No problem." Jean pulled herself away from the cold wall and thought, *she doesn't have red hair at all.*

She had dark ringlets around a face so pale her puffy, brightly patterned coat looked like a tea cozy nestling an egg. Her eyes were also dark, and seemed to be spilling down her rounded cheeks. . . . No, she'd been crying, and her copious if carefully applied make-up had smeared and run. She peered frantically from Alasdair to Jean and back but slumped rather than struggled.

Up the steps galloped two constables, one man, one woman. "Here," said the former, this time in reproof.

The latter said, "We're only trying to help, Miss Herries. Amy."

"Herries?" Alasdair repeated under his breath. "Sara Herries?"

"Yeh," Amy said. "My sister was Sara Herries. Yesterday's news, eh? Out of sight, out of mind."

Not necessarily, Jean thought. Edinburgh had never been Alasdair's patch, but an unsolved missing person case would have crossed his desk in Inverness.

The two constables removed Amy from Alasdair's grasp and, everyone jockeying carefully around the landing, aimed her up the stairs. "Thank you kindly, sir," said the man to Alasdair.

Alasdair didn't have to say anything about force of habit. His "Carry on, Constable," proclaimed his former profession as clearly as if he wore a name tag.

From the nether regions came the same astringent voice, its low register reverberating in the stairwell. "Take her to the station, give her tea, I'll be along presently."

"Tea and no sympathy," muttered Amy, but she allowed herself to be steered up the steps and away. A murmur of interest greeted her at the outside door.

"Cameron?" inquired the disembodied voice, less a spirit of the ancient world, Jean thought, than D.I. Knox in female person. She'd never have assumed an academic was male, and heaven knew she'd met enough distaff police people she should have left her options open—but then, Alasdair, too, had assumed the Detective Inspector was a man.

"Oh aye," Alasdair called, apparently unmoved by his mistake. "Just coming."

Jean had thought it was cold and stuffy upstairs. Every step downwards, however, carried her deeper into an ominous chilly stillness.

Chapter Three

The cellar might be every bit as dank as Jean had—not feared, she reassured herself, anticipated—but it wasn't as dark. Several bulbs glared down from the rough-hewn beams of the ceiling, illuminating the spiky red hair of D.I. Knox.

Oh. The constable had been referring not to Amy Herries, but to this, this Valkyrie. She had to be close to six feet tall, four inches taller than Alasdair. She stepped forward, hand extended, eyes hooded in a face as beautifully carved as a Renaissance sculpture. "Wendy Knox."

Wendy? Jean thought. No telling what teasing about Peter Pan and Tinkerbelle this poor woman had suffered from her male colleagues, all the more because of her stature.

With practiced expressionlessness, Alasdair shook her hand. "Hullo. This is Jean Fairbairn, from *Great Scot* magazine. My wife."

Jean let Knox's cold hand engulf and release hers, tilting her head back to look the woman in her cosmetic-free hazel eyes. She not only towered over Jean's five-foot-three, she outweighed her by several stone. Not that she was fat. As far as Jean could tell, Knox's body was all lean muscle and taut tendon beneath a stylish dark pants suit, its severity lightened by a necklace of multicolored agates and gold hoop earrings.

Jean tried a smile. "Don't worry, I write travel and history articles, I'm not a reporter, not exactly."

"American, are you? A bit cheeky, then, to be writing about Scotland."

So the Inspector believed the best defense was offense. No need to get offended, though. Jean stood as straight as she could without rising onto her tiptoes, smoothed the naturally surly tendrils of her own hair, and said with an even wider smile, "I've been doing a fish out of water number. Or a fish leaping out of one water into another."

"I know what you do," Knox replied. "The both of you. You've been involved in a few homicide cases this last year, haven't you now?"

"Oh aye," said Alasdair. "What's this about the Herries case? Any chance your body is the missing woman's?"

"The cow," Knox said, an upward flick of her eyes dismissing Amy. "She was making a wild guess is all. That newspaper article's attracted too much interest." This time her gaze flicked toward Jean.

Jean didn't bother with another smile. She might be her brother's keeper, but she couldn't keep her brethren at *The Scotsman* from a scoop.

"What's the medical examiner saying?" Alasdair asked.

"He's downstairs now. Have a look for yourselves."

Oh good, Jean thought. *I was so hoping you'd say that.*

Knox strode briskly away across the stone pavement. Alasdair looked around at Jean. "You can be waiting for me at Blackwell's. Or get yourself back to the office, and I'll phone."

"No way. I'm coming, too."

"Aye?" he asked.

"Yeah, well, since when has my claustrophobia outweighed my curiosity?"

"Never, not so's I've noticed. Come along then."

Jean went along, looking around the cellar like a condemned man taking in his last sight of freedom. But the subterranean room looked reassuringly mundane. All four corners had been cleared. Old furniture, more junk than antique—though you never knew—was stacked near the staircase along with collapsing cardboard boxes and lumps that could just as well be trolls as trash bags. What part of the central floor wasn't piled with the remains of lives long gone displayed a collection of tools, lumber, a couple of sawhorses— all contributions to the new pub upstairs. And, Jean thought as she spotted a wooden platform taking shape against the far wall, contributions to a stage down here.

Pipes. Plumbers. Between the beams of the ceiling, the flooring of the building above, snaked a maze of pipes large and small. Most were scabrous metal, their joints arthritic with age, but several were modern PVC. An army might march on its stomach, thought Jean, but a pub surely ran on its plumbing. No wonder the hapless plumbers had been down here poking into the walls.

Now it was Knox who stood beside a rough, rectangular hole. Stones and scraps of mortar were piled around the base of a nearby police-issue light stanchion. Two coveralled crime scene technicians squatted on their haunches near its halo of light, either searching for clues such as footprints or cigarette butts or taking their ease. One of them grinned. "No rush, Inspector. Those puir bodies'll no be away for a dauner afore you get there."

The other fingered the shining screen of his smartphone and muttered, "You'd best be unrolling a ball of string, you'll no be getting a signal in those catacombs."

"Thank you kindly," said Knox over her shoulder and, no doubt, through her teeth.

Alasdair had pulled a small flashlight from his coat pocket and was inspecting the impromptu doorway. Except, Jean saw in the traveling blotch of light, it wasn't impromptu at all. The pattern of the stones changed from the squared blocks of the wall to irregularly shaped rocks mortared into a stone-framed rectangle. "There was a door here already," she said.

"There was that," Alasdair replied, and to Knox, "The plumbers punched through just here, I reckon, because the rubble fill would be easier to shift than knocking a hole in the wall itself. But why? Where they meaning to connect with the mains beneath the street? Seems to me there's many a pipe already here—the building's had access to the mains all this time."

"I've been asking that as well," Knox replied. "The plumbers and the manager of the pub, a chap named Bewley, will be giving me an answer. In any event, they knocked out enough of the rubble to step through. We opened it up further, when they got a bit more than they bargained for."

Did they? Jean asked herself, remembering Miranda's, *The*

owner of the new pub likely ordered the tradesmen to ca' down the wall, the better to increase his trade.

Alasdair shone his light into the pitch blackness beyond the opening. Knox picked up a nearby industrial-strength flashlight and did the same. Jean peered past them both, to see nothing but a small stone chamber and steps plunging even further downward.

She took a step backward, then forced her feet to carry her forward again, to where her sleeve touched Alasdair's. So far she wasn't sensing anything emanating from the hole other than stale air and mildew, its wet-dog stench making the last trace of the stairwell's fresh paint seem like perfume. Not that she was taking deep breaths. Her ribs seemed to be closing around her lungs like an iron maiden.

"That's why you're consulting with P&S, because we've got detailed plans of all these buildings and the vaults beneath," Alasdair said to Knox. "Though I've not yet had time to see if this entrance, this area, is in the records."

"You'll be letting me know, then." Her flashlight before her like a lance, Knox stepped through the doorway. "I'd also like your opinion on the bodies. Shall we?"

Let's not, said a little voice in the back of Jean's mind. She hooked her elbow around Alasdair's free arm, and told his inquiring glance, "If the lights go out I want to make sure it's you I'm hanging onto."

He must have read the same article on relationships. Rather than rolling his eyes, he nodded gravely and pressed her arm against his side. Together they stepped into the catacomb.

Following the unwavering beam of Knox's flashlight, they picked their way down a stairwell so constricted the two of them had to press even more tightly together. The narrow stone steps were gritty beneath Jean's shoes. She touched the scabrous plaster of the wall with her free hand to steady herself, and her skin crawled at the cold, damp, slime-over-sandpaper surface. The reek of mold and mildew had an elusive aftertaste of smoke, trapped here beneath the city since the fire of 2002 or even since the occupancy of over a century ago.

Down, down, one flight of steps, a landing, an angle, another flight of steps—surely they were approaching the center of the Earth and a dinosaur was about the burst through the walls, walls which were not closing in . . . No, Jean told herself firmly, they were only approaching the level of the Cowgate, the street that crossed under the South Bridge, and the walls had not moved.

Suddenly the steps ended, the walls seemed to fall away, and Knox's light illuminated a corridor. The rooms opening to either side were no more than ink-black voids, except for one, its arched opening outlined by glare. *Lights, camera, action.*

Jean caught a cautious gleam from Alasdair's blue eyes, and knew that he, too, was—well, the word wasn't quite *listening.* Letting his extra and not entirely welcome sense take in whatever paranormal resonances vibrated gently and invisibly between air and shadow.

She raised her eyebrows in a query. *Getting anything?*

He shook his head.

No, the place was oppressive, sad, tired. But not haunted. Not just now, anyway.

Knox strolled on into the doorway of the illuminated chamber and beckoned the two laggards. Still hanging onto Alasdair—a literal pratfall on Ramsay Lane was nothing compared to a perceptual pratfall here—Jean squinted into the light.

The chamber's barrel-vaulted roof, black with soot, dipped close to the gravelly floor on right and left. Rough brick-and-mortar shelving ranged up the far, flat end. A dark blotch of moisture stained one wall. The room was empty except for a coffin-shaped network of metal strips in one corner and a human-shaped lumpy mass in the center, illuminated much too well by the operating-room glare from a couple of light stanchions. Two men crouched beside it, one in coveralls, one in a trench coat.

The latter stood up, and up, and up. He was even taller than Knox, but less wide, a flesh-and-blood version of *Star Wars'* C3P-O. Simultaneously cringing and dodging as his swept-back hair brushed the ceiling, he turned the axe-blade of his nose toward Knox. "You've come back then, have you?"

"You're needing supervising?" Knox retorted, and, without looking around at Jean and Alasdair, "D.S. Gordon. Mr. Cameron of Protect and Survive. His wife, Miss Fairbairn of *Great Scot.*"

Gordon held out his hand, realized he was wearing latex gloves, and settled for a brisk nod. "*Great Scot?*"

"I'm only here observing," Jean told him.

"There's many a muckle to be observing. This here's a woman, Dr. Kazmarek's saying."

The other man made a vague gesture of acknowledgment and kept on plying his collection bags and tweezers. Jean managed to inch forward without releasing Alasdair, so that the lights weren't reflecting off the smudges on her glasses, and observed.

Ashes to ashes, dust to dust—this body was clay to clay. It was hard to believe that all those dun-colored clumps and furrows had once been flesh and blood. Now its—*her*—garments were no more than threads melded to leathery bits of skin and protruding angles of bone. Her face was turned toward the door, eye sockets filled with fibrous matter that might be spider webs, or might be memories.

Her jaw hung slackly open. Jean knew that it was natural for the jaw to drop after death, but still, the gaping mouth seemed to scream, as though the woman had lain here watching light retreat up the staircase and devouring darkness ooze from the depths.

Or had someone carried the last vestige of light and life away up the steps? Perhaps she'd come here alone, lost in the labyrinth beneath the city, or, despondent, had chosen here to lie down and die.

Something echoed deep in the profound silence of the grave, and Jean looked sharply around. But she heard only a slow drip of water that, magnified by the stone corridors, had for a moment sounded like footsteps.

The pressure of Alasdair's arm counseled, *Steady on.* In the light his face was calm, lead shielding fully raised. He asked, "Is this Sara Herries? Or perhaps we should be asking, if it's not Sara Herries, who is it, then?"

Knox was hanging back by the doorway, her arms folded tightly across the chest of her coat, the huge flashlight tucked beneath her arm. Either she'd gone a bit paler, or her already fair skin was blanched by the harsh light. What? Jean wondered. Was she queasy around death? For a detective, that would be a handicap akin to a sailor being seasick.

When Knox didn't answer, Gordon said. "It's early days yet. We'll be collecting evidence, estimating her age, looking out a cause of death that'll show up in the bones . . ."

Alasdair said, "Perhaps I should be introducing myself a bit further, Sergeant. Detective Chief Inspector Alasdair Cameron, Northern Constabulary, retired."

"Ah. Well then. I'm teaching my grandmother to suck eggs, eh?"

Alasdair's "No problem," didn't stop Gordon from darting a resentful glance at Knox.

One corner of Knox's mouth puckered, perhaps in a smile at Gordon's discomfiture. This, Jean thought, was not a team made in heaven.

D.S. Gordon's dark coat was dusty around the hem, as were his shoes and the trousers of his suit. Knox's black pumps were almost pristine, as though she'd flown through the wet streets rather than walked. His accent was Aberdonian, sounding like a mouthful of thistles. Edinburgh accents were milder than Aberdeen's—or Glasgow's, or even Alasdair's delicious western Highland brogue—but still Knox sounded more generalized British than Scottish. Was she not a local lass? Had she attended a posh girl's school in England? Miranda had attended a posh girl's school in England, and could do Received Pronunciation just fine, but she still spoke Scots when at home . . .

Well, if there was some sort of class or locality static between Gordon and Knox, it was none of Jean's business. The vault was. Now.

Chapter Four

Gordon squatted back down in the scuffed mud, grit, and gravel, this time inspecting the contents of several plastic bins. "There's no handbag or the like, nothing to ID the body, though someone's dropped a penny dated 1994 in the corridor."

"Most obliging, then, of whoever was here since then," Knox said.

"Never minding the blocked door," Alasdair added. "That matches with Amy Herries saying fifteen years. And with Sara going missing just here, although 'just here' could mean the university area, or the Old Town." He looked around at Knox. *Your turn.*

"She disappeared in July of 1996, was last seen late at night, at a club just two doors closer to the High Street, with her boyfriend. He went missing as well, and the police supposed she ran away with him."

"Is he the other body?" asked Alasdair.

Oh yeah, Jean thought. The plumbers, or spelunkers, whatever, found two bodies. But where . . .

"Not likely." With a groan, Kazmarek rose to his feet. He was a bulky man, and almost bald—in his coveralls he looked like a high-browed Beluga whale. One latex-covered hand indicated the largest of the blue plastic bins. "That's a disarticulated skeleton, probably much older than this one, though it's hard to distinguish age under any condition, let alone these."

As one, Jean and Alasdair leaned over to look. No, those brown sticks and clods weren't more rubble, but were ribs, arm bones, the small joints of fingers, all piled neatly atop foam rubber padding much like the padding that had protected the components of Jean's new computer. The smooth dome of a cranium sat at one end, face down, inert.

Funny, how the more the body looked like an anatomical specimen, the less chilling it was to see. And yet that cranium had held thoughts and dreams just as surely as the one beneath the lights. As the living ones beneath the lights.

Cold seeped upward through Jean's shoes, and in through her coat everywhere except where she pressed against Alasdair, and even down through the roots of her hair. If the lights were emitting any warmth, it wasn't enough to drive back two centuries of chill.

"This one's a man. There're no associated artifacts except for a few buttons and those." Kazmarek's toe stirred a smaller bin the size of a shoe box.

Alasdair bent closer, pulling Jean with him. Any other time she'd have abandoned the Siamese twin routine, but not now. The ceiling was not pressing down, she told herself. The stairwell was not closing like a throat swallowing.

In the box lay a rectangular pile of what looked like sheets of pastry piled one on the other and then merged into one decayed mass. The top layer might be leather—it looked more like decayed skin than the real thing. Strips of something black bracketed one side. "It's a book," she said. "With the embossed cover and what might be silver clasps, probably a Bible. There are conservators at the Museum of Scotland who could work magic with that."

"A Bible, is it? That's a crucifix, I reckon." Gordon indicated two small lengths of wood that might once have been glued together.

"A cross," said Jean. "A crucifix would have a figure of Christ. Unless there was one that fell off."

"Oh," Gordon returned. "Well then."

Were the tiny striations in the leather binding of the book and the wood of the cross tooth marks? The objects were both so eaten by time and decay Jean couldn't tell if they'd also been eaten by rats. She didn't look back at the bones, either set of them. Rats. Worms. Insects. *We're all eaten by worms and insects, but rats, now, no, not rats.* She shivered.

Alasdair, not at all fooled, glanced at her. "Almost time for you to be leaving?" he whispered.

"Almost. Not quite." Louder, she asked the air, since Knox was still behind her, "Are there any stories about this—well, I guess not this particular vault, since no one knew it was here. Or knew for sure it was here, anyway. About this building or the ones around it?"

"Stories?" asked Knox, from what seemed like a long way away.

Loosening her grip of Alasdair, Jean turned toward her. "The kind of stories you hear all up and down the South Bridge. I mean, the bar upstairs is called The Resurrectionist for a reason. Supposedly body snatchers like Burke and Hare operated down here as well as in the cheap boarding houses and pubs. They didn't just steal the bodies of people no one would miss, they created bodies of ditto. But why return a body to vaults after it was dissected by Dr. . . . Oh. Well, his name was Robert Knox."

"Knox?" A tremor went over Gordon's face—apparently he was fighting back a grin.

Wendy Knox didn't grin. She didn't so much as twitch. She was probably used to standing her ground on this issue, too. "Yes, Burke and Hare sold bodies to a Dr. Knox at the university. He should have been hanged as well, I expect, as an enabler, at the least, but he was never even tried."

"Justice system wasn't so different then," muttered Gordon. "The ordinary folk do what needs doing to get by, the rich folk profit."

He and Knox might be having a socio-economic clash, Jean told herself, and went on, "What about other stories, you know, about ghosts and things going bump in the darkness? Human figures seeming to walk through walls, or going into rooms with no exit and not coming out. Things moved around. Odd scratches. The lights going out."

She saw Knox staring at her. She sensed Gordon and Kazmarek staring at her, and at Alasdair as well, who was doing his great-stone-face act.

The lights went out.

Jean knew her eyes were open as wide as they'd go, she could feel dust gathering on her irises. She could feel the darkness itself, a palpable presence, choking her . . .

The lights flared. They'd probably no more than blinked— certainly there had been no time for Knox or Alasdair to switch on their flashlights. Jean realized she had both arms wrapped around Alasdair's arm. His hand was probably turning blue. She loosened her grip.

"Breathe," he murmured, his warm breath tickling her ear.

Oh. Yeah. She forced a few molecules of trapped air out of her chest, then sucked another few in. At her feet, on the woman's body, something caught the light and emitted a furtive sparkle. A bit of jewelry, sunk deep into the rotted flesh.

"I've not asked about ghost stories." Knox's voice was a cool and calm as though nothing had happened, but she now held the flashlight like a truncheon in front of her. And Jean could have sworn the woman was now three feet closer to the staircase, calling into the room from the corridor. "Ghost stories aren't evidence."

"They are for Jean." Alasdair's voice dropped into a lower register. "Yon dismembered body might be dating back to Burke and Hare—when, Jean?"

"1820s," she said, her voice sounding to her own ears as though she'd just gulped helium. But no one seemed to notice. She tried again. "The Anatomy Act of 1832 made it easier for doctors to obtain donated bodies, so the resurrectionist trade pretty much died out."

Alasdair nodded. "So why's this body, donated or not, still lying about? Folk were in and out of these vaults until the late nineteenth century. Or, if the body's got nothing to do with body snatchers, if it's been here longer than twenty years but less than a hundred or so, how did it get in here? How did the woman's body get in here, come to that? Was the door opened up and then re-mortared? Is there any way of testing the mortar, seeing how old it is? Or is there another way in?"

Knox opened her mouth as if to speak, perhaps to protest

that Alasdair was getting all the good lines, but Kazmarek spoke first. "That's for you lot to decide. Just one more thing before we pack it all up and carry it away. What's that metal contraption? Not a chicken coop, I'm thinking. I know people were living in these vaults, but chickens?"

His latex hand, smooth as an alien's, swept toward the bottomless oblong box of interlaced metal strips. Iron strips—their surfaces were crumbling with rust. Jean waited politely, but no one else offered any answers.

"Well," she said, hoping she wasn't coming across as teacher's pet, "speaking of Burke and Hare and their ilk, this is a mortsafe. Or most of one, anyway. You know, 'mort' as in 'mortality' or 'mortuary'? People would lock a mortsafe over the grave of a loved one, to keep the body snatchers from getting to it until, ah, the body was no longer desirable."

Silence, and four faces turned toward her, their expressions ranging from nonplussed to intrigued.

"You see them in museums every now and then," Jean went on. "There are a couple just over in Greyfriars Kirkyard. They were more or less for the wealthy. Poorer people would sometimes pile large stones on top of the grave, or arrange pebbles in a certain pattern. Although if you found the pattern disturbed, what could you do? Go down to the nearest medical school and ask for your relative's bits and pieces back again?"

Six faces, she decided, counting those of the dead.

No surprise Alasdair recovered first. "If a mortsafe's something you'd be finding in a kirkyard . . ."

This time Knox interrupted. "Why's one here? And what, if anything, has it to do with these bodies? What, come to that, have these bodies to do with each other?"

"You've got quite the cold case here," Alasdair told her.

Literally, Jean thought with another shiver. "Tell you what. I'm going to leave y'all with it. Miranda's expecting me at the office. She's arranged an interview with the owner of the property."

"Well then," said Knox, "best you go asking *him* about the local ghost stories."

Kazmarek peeled off his gloves. So did Gordon. Together they started putting lids on the bins. "Give my lads up the stairs a shout, if you please," the doctor told Jean. "We'll be obliged to shift the larger body to the morgue in a larger box."

"I'd be glad to," Jean said as Alasdair escorted her out of the chamber—really, the ceiling was starting to sag, she was sure of it, and her ears rang from silence between voices and breaths and scuffle of feet.

She did not look back at the woman's body, the vacant eyes staring toward the stairwell. Jean hoped she'd been dead before she came here. Before she'd been abandoned here. She hoped the woman would be identified, as Sara Herries or as someone else, and her remains returned to relatives. She hoped the entirety of the cold case would be solved, the woman, the man, the mortsafe, and not just because she wanted to know what had happened.

Hoping she wouldn't have nightmares, she paused at the foot of the stairs, looking right and left into the shadowed tunnel. In one direction it seemed to end at a wall—at least the darkness took on substantiality there, just beyond the rim of light. In the other direction, the corridor vanished into an infinite void. She imagined people living here, choking on their own smoke, their own waste.

"I didn't exactly cover myself with glory, cowering against you the entire time," she told Alasdair, even as her feet itched for the treads and the upward scramble.

"Needs must. You redeemed yourself by answering a good many questions."

"That's not redemption. That's being a know-it-all."

"That as well," he said, and she suspected he wasn't joking. "It's best you . . ." He stopped, darting a glance over his shoulder.

Knox had stepped back into the doorway and stood, hands on hips, shoulders stiff, watching Kazmarek and Gordon at their work. But the sound of footsteps wasn't coming from them.

Jean felt the all-too-familiar blanket of perception settling down onto her already lead-weighted shoulders, and the back of her neck prickling to an ectoplasmic kiss. She felt Alasdair's shudder, his breath going suddenly ragged.

From the depth of shadow walked a pale figure. She was no more than colorless mist in human shape, shoes rising and falling two inches above the lumps of the floor, an apron covering a long skirt, a wide collar over a bodice with two hands folded demurely in front, neat little bonnet atop a face that was two dark splotches and a mouth set in calm determination.

The figure walked past Knox's back, one elbow actually passing through her jacket. Knox stirred uneasily, but didn't look around.

Jean's and Alasdair's faces turned to follow the—young woman, not just a figure, the ghost of a human life—down the corridor into the darkness. She vanished into the blank, black face of the wall with only the slightest trace of a shimmer, less substantial than the shapes behind the windows of the coffee bars on the High Street.

Jean straightened. Alasdair shook himself. They looked at each other. "Right," he said, well beneath his breath.

"Seventeenth-century clothing."

"No sense her walking an eighteenth-century tunnel, then."

"Is she connected to the cold case? Or is it time for something completely different? Is she walking toward the street, toward the South Bridge, or away from it—I've usually got a good sense of direction, but down here . . ."

"Where's this corridor go?" Alasdair asked Knox.

"Nowhere. There are walls in both directions."

"Ta." Alasdair smiled, if thinly. He produced his flashlight, switched it on, and handed it to Jean. "Up you go, and away to work. I'll phone."

"Yeah. You do that." Jean essayed a smile of her own, squeezed his arm one last time, and turned to the stairwell. The small firefly of light wavered in front of her. *No, don't run, you could slip and fall.*

Step, step, step—there was a glow ahead—*cellar door*, yeah that was a beautiful sound—she almost did an Amy Herries into one of the technicians, who'd chosen that exact moment to peer inquisitively through the rough doorway and down the stairs.

Jean apologized and pushed past him into the vast, spacious reaches of the cellar, just as he apologized and dodged. She didn't stop, just threw, "Dr. Kazmarek wants y'all down there, he's ready to move the body," over her shoulder as she sped toward and then up the newer stairwell with its ambrosial odor of fresh paint.

The upper hallway was now brightly lit, and the door to the pub stood open, emitting more beautiful light and the sounds of nail gun and power saw. That's why the lights in the vault had blinked, a sudden surge in demand for electricity had addled the building's antique electric nervous system.

A hint of sawdust in the air tickled her nose and she sneezed, expelling the odor of decay, then sneezed again.

A heavy-set man wearing a hard hat surged out of the doorway like a cuckoo out of a clock. "Eh! Are you the female detective? How long's your lot taking up space in the cellar and holding up progress? To say nothing of questioning me as though I've done something wrong."

"I'm not Inspector Knox, she's still down—downstairs. I'm Jean Fairbairn." She didn't owe him any explanations of why she was there. "Are you Mr. Bewley, the manager?"

"Oh aye, muggins here is the manager, having no worse motive than doing a day's work for a day's pay." Beady brown eyes peered out from the shadow of the hat, assessing Jean, dismissing her, and focusing on the door to the stairwell. His full lips tightened in their nest of three-day-old whiskers, an effect he probably meant to be stylish but which Jean's inner schoolmarm assessed and then dismissed as sloppy. His casual grooming didn't mean the pub's glasses would be dirty or the packets of crisps crushed, but the slight aroma of alcohol on his breath didn't inspire confidence.

"D.I. Knox is just doing her job, too," Jean said, heading

for the door. *So is Alasdair. So am I.*

She burst out onto the street to see that it was no longer raining. Behind the thick clouds, the sun had to be shining gloriously. Even with the scent of diesel and old fry-ups, the air seemed free and clear.

The crowd had dispersed, presumably when the squad car departed, leaving the constable of the "red-headed hellion" comment in command of the field. Jean supposed Amy had gone with the car. Poor thing. Crying was a legitimate response to stress, although she could have timed her tears better. She wouldn't get any sympathy from the likes of Knox, who in proving she was as good as any man couldn't allow herself to cut another woman any slack.

The constable in his shiny jacket the color of key-lime pie stood at parade rest. In the shadow of his cap, his reddened nose turned to track two young women whose backpacks and bulbous coats made their legs clad in colorful tights look even longer and slimmer. The duo headed off toward the university, either not noticing or not caring they were under scrutiny. Jean remembered one of Hugh's jokes, a woman's response to a flirtatious male: *You die trying, I'll die laughing.*

Yes, with his reddened nose, the constable seemed less Rudolph Valentino than Rudolph the Reindeer.

Suppressing her smile, Jean looked past him. A gap on either side of the street revealed that it really was a bridge spanning the medieval lane—the cow path—of the Cowgate. Beyond the opening gleamed the blue-painted front of Blackwell's Bookshop, its gravitational pull tugging at her as surely as that of a High Street coffee bar. But no. Business now, pleasure later.

She turned ninety degrees to consider Lady Niddry's House across the street. Unlike almost every other building on the South Bridge, including the one she stood in front of, it didn't have a contemporary but a—restored, Jean assumed—classical facade and portico in that mock Greco-Roman style she'd always found cold and distant. Above the portico, damp stains and bits of moss like green hedgehogs hiding in crevices softened its elegant but stern lines.

Something was different . . . That was it. The somewhat shorter windows of what she'd have called the second floor, but which here in the UK was designated the first, sported a new sign. No longer did an understated script black on white panel read "Lady Niddry's Closet", a posh shop that had been one of Miranda's haunts. Now a small but vivid crimson signboard read, "Pippa's Erotic Gear".

Whatever "erotic gear" was. Jean suspected items that would be uncomfortable if not downright embarrassing. But then, to some people the voluminous skirts of the eighteenth-century served as erotic inspiration. Personally, she though Alasdair's kilt was pretty darned erotic.

What she'd at first thought was a mannequin behind the window glass moved. At that distance, Jean could see the woman's clothing, an electric blue skin-tight jacket and pants with a sheen that suggested vinyl, more clearly than she could see her face, a ghostly blur beneath what was much more likely a smooth fall of fair hair than a nun-like veil. A blur that was tilted either toward Jean herself or the constable she stood beside.

Her stance reminded Jean of Wendy Knox's, straight, firm, arms akimbo with a habit of command. She couldn't be the owner—Miranda had already said the owner was Vasudev Prasad and her own Duncan Kerr. A sales clerk?

"Ah, her," said the constable, and Jean jerked around, startled. But the man had already proved he could speak, not to mention observe. "She's been watching most all this time, even before the car drew a crowd. Not enough trade to be keeping her interest, I reckon, even with the chap from here stopping by for a blether, the both of them side by side in the window like no one could be seeing in, and she giving him laldy good and proper."

"Bewley, the manager of The Resurrectionist?" Jean asked. "She was angry with him?"

"Chap needing a shave and an attitude adjustment? Aye, that's him. Came slinking back this way less an organ or two, if you take my meaning."

She took his meaning. "Well, both buildings are owned by the same people, so I guess when Bewley called in the police . . . Who did call in the police? Bewley? Or the plumbers who found the bodies?"

"Not a clue, madam. They told me off to stand here and keep the gawpers away is all."

Amy Herries rated a "Miss". Jean rated a "Madam". Go figure.

She glanced back at Lady Niddry's. The woman had vanished, leaving the window to a spotlighted wooden library ladder. Various items hung from its steps, something feathery, something leathery, and something consisting of silvery chain links. Not one hint of tartan. But Jean supposed the locals were less likely to fantasize about kilts.

"Thanks," she told the constable, and nodded to his mock-salute.

Sending a moment's thought toward Alasdair, somewhere in the catacombs beneath her feet, she headed back to the High Street and her familiar paper- and coffee-scented office.

Chapter Five

Jean barely had time to hang up her coat, comb her hair, and gratefully accept a café latte from Gavin, child-receptionist and aspiring barista, before Miranda pounced.

Today she was wearing an intricate Aran sweater over a white blouse, black trousers, and cowboy boots, their leather tooled with Texas bluebonnets and Scottish thistles. "Time to be putting me in the picture, Jean."

"Good grief, let me dry out and thaw out," Jean told her, trying not to gulp and burn her mouth. *Ahhh.* Caffeine, milkfat, and warmth. No more mildew and death clotting her throat.

Miranda had the much larger office, but then, as editor-in-chief and publisher she had the much larger responsibility, Jean being less silent partner than stealth collaborator. The sleek Swedish-style furnishings exposed a corner here and a soffit there, but were mostly buried beneath stacks of books, papers, files, and souvenirs from many a jaunt around the globe. The seeming disarray set Jean's teeth on edge, but then, by the time she could locate a book or document in her meticulously organized office, Miranda would be standing there with two copies, tapping her foot impatiently.

Moving a stack of competitors' current issues off a chair, she sat down and between sips put Miranda in the picture.

"Well, well, well," was the predictable response. "It's a cold case, then, within *Great Scot's* brief. Better than true crime."

"Better than having a body drop at your feet," Jean said, with feeling. "Better than finding someone you know dead."

"Someone knew the dead folk. Amy, it sounds like."

"The woman might be Sara, yes, but the man doesn't seem to be her boyfriend. It looks like someone from an earlier era." Jean didn't mention her and Alasdair's ghost-sighting. Not that Miranda wouldn't be interested. It was just that until she—

they—found some sort of corroborating evidence, a story, forensics, something, then the ghost didn't count as a clue, only as a memory without an anchor. She cautioned, "In fact, there might not be any sort of crime at all. A puzzle, but not a crime."

"In the legal sense." Miranda leaned back in her chair. The self-effacing blond hairdo she'd worn for Jean and Alasdair's wedding right after New Year's was now an even more mild-mannered honey-brown, softening her keenly intelligent face.

Jean wondered how long it would be before that honey-brown segued into, say, auburn streaks or even red spikes like Knox's. "Did you know that Lady Niddry's Closet, across the street, is now Pippa's Erotic Gear?"

"Oh aye. Duncan's saying that's more appropriate to the area, university lasses less interested in business attire than in having themselves a good time. Than in their boyfriends' having a good time as well. More's the pity—about the shopping, that is, not the good times. There are more than enough clothing shops in town."

"The restaurant downstairs, Lady Niddry's Drawing Room, is still open, isn't it?"

"That it is. You'll not be finding another setting like that elsewhere in the city, a drawing room with a dungeon below, a modern kitchen serving up the finest in Scottish cuisine."

"No need to sell it to me," Jean said with a laugh. "We'll make it there eventually. Neither of us find eating out quite the sport some people do."

Miranda, under no relationship cautions, not after all these years, rolled her eyes. But before she could launch into her spiel about restaurants as vital cogs in the wheels of society as well as purveyors of food, the outer door opened and shut and Gavin's voice echoed down the hallway. "Good morning to you, sir. Mr. Prasad, is it?"

"Yes, quite," man's voice replied.

"May I take your coat, sir? Fancy a coffee? Espresso?"

"An espresso would come a treat, there's a good lad."

"I'm after brewing a fresh lot just now, sir, for Mir—, ah,

Ms. Capaldi's elevenses. Half a tick."

"Gavin is wasted at reception." Miranda rose from her chair and headed for the door. "He'd make a fine maitre d' at Lady Niddry's Drawing Room. Vasudev! So glad you could come calling on such short notice!"

The man she waved into her office had the body of a teddy bear, short, round, and soft, encased in a pinstriped suit that even fashion-impaired Jean recognized as the product of an exclusive tailor. His black hair and black moustache, rich brown complexion, and even richer brown eyes betrayed his roots far from Scotland's shores, but his accent placed his personal point of origin near the shores of the English Channel. "Good morning to you, Miranda. And this would be Miss Fairbairn, I expect."

"It's Jean. Good to meet you." Jean stood up, shook hands—for a big man, his grip was surprisingly diffident—and moved to the back corner of the room. By the time Miranda seated Vasudev and resumed her perch behind her desk, Jean had removed a nest of Russian dolls from a second chair and pulled her trusty, low-tech notebook and pencil from her mini-backpack.

She squelched a giggle when Miranda leaned forward, planted her elbows on the desk and steepled her fingertips—the detective was on the case. "Well then, Vasudev. What's this I'm hearing? Bodies turning up in the cellar of the Playfair Building?"

He shrugged. "You know as much as I do, Miranda."

Actually, Jean thought, she knew a lot more.

"I gather a couple of tradesmen were removing a century's worth of rubbish from the cellar," Vasudev continued, "all the better to remodel the area, insert toilets, and so on, and they discovered a blocked-up door. The manager, Des Bewley, took it upon himself to have them investigate. Enterprising lad, Bewley. I'd have done the same, had I been on the premises at the time. The vaults beneath the South Bridge are quite the tourist attraction."

Miranda sent a subtle smirk toward Jean. *Right yet again, a matter of marketing not sewage.*

Jean nodded graciously.

"When they turned up the bodies, though, it became a police matter. So I dutifully rang the police."

"Before or after you rang *The Scotsman?*" asked Miranda.

Vasudev's smile was a crescent of gleaming white teeth. "After, of course. I didn't want the police telling me to keep it quiet, did I now?"

"Not at all."

"Besides, it's not so much a police matter as one for an archaeologist. Or perhaps for Miss Fair—Jean, here, with her articles on history and legend."

Jean hadn't intended asking about ghost stories, not quite so quickly, anyway, but neither did she intend passing up an opening. "Are there ghost stories about that building?"

"Odd that you should ask that." Vasudev frowned slightly.

The door opened, and the aroma of coffee preceded Gavin into the room. He unerringly found the one empty spot on Miranda's desk large enough for the tray and set it down. "Here you are, sir. Miranda. Jean, you've already got your latte, but I can be topping it up . . ."

"I'm fine, thanks," Jean said, but didn't refuse the offered plate of cookies. Chocolate covered digestive biscuits helped to keep the dark and the cold at bay. And right now she didn't mean the weather.

Gavin, she noted, was either using what she knew to be a modest salary to buy clothing that fit him, or else he was growing into his hand-me-down suit. "That all right for you, then?" he asked.

"Ta," Miranda told him, and he disappeared out the door, to the sound of the phone ringing on his desk.

"Quite an interesting bit of gender reversal you've got here," Vasudev said. "In my office, it's the girls who bring the coffee."

"I'm sure they do," Miranda told him, tones crisp as her blouse, and moved on. "Jean was asking about ghost stories."

"Mind you, I've never seen anything at all uncanny in

either the Playfair Building or at Lady Niddry's. Not unless you count the rows amongst the kitchen staff, voices like Macbeth's witches, some of those women have . . ." Carefully holding his plate so as to keep crumbs from falling on his paisley-pattern tie and pocket square, Vasudev took a bite of biscuit and chewed. ". . . but supposedly a waiter took to his heels last year when a ghost fell from the landing at the top of the main staircase bang in front of him."

"He could see ghosts," Jean said.

Vasudev shrugged. "It's all rumor. I expect the kitchen staff was simply trying to cover up for his abrupt departure for some personal reason. Young people these days have so little loyalty to their employers."

Jean wrote, "Ghost at L Niddry's? Gender?" in her notebook. "Why is it odd I should ask?"

"That American telly presenter, Jason Pagano, rang my office—let me see, it was just this Tuesday, day before yesterday. He didn't say where he heard the story, but he wants to include Lady Niddry's in his program. Could be he had a word with Bewley as well, leading to the present sequence of events."

Oh? Jean wrote "Jason Pagano rears his head!"

"Program? American chap? There are many ghost-hunting programs these days, codswallop draped in scientific jiggery-pokery, if you're asking me. Like that Mystic Scotland woman." Miranda favored Jean with a sideways glance.

"Very much so," agreed Vasudev, over the rim of his cup. "Naught but innuendo and sensationalism. Although Mystic Scotland's obviously filling a marketing niche, and quite successfully."

"Mystic Scotland is supernatural lite," Jean said. "Hippy dippy rainbows and unicorns. Pagano's something else again. His 'Beyond the Edge' is into vampires and violence. Evil spirits, poltergeists, a stake and a cross. Ghost stories aren't necessarily horror stories, but it's the horror that's his subject matter. Suitably embellished, of course."

"I've often wondered, wouldn't a spirit have to be

Christian in order to be dissuaded by a cross?"

"Well, yeah." She remembered the sad wooden bits of what might have been a cross lying near the male body.

"Do you believe in evil spirits, Miss Fair—Jean?" Vasudev's eyes, dark as the espresso in his cup, focused unblinking on Jean. Miranda, face downcast, picked grains of sugar off the cookie plate with a manicured fingertip.

"In evil, yes. In spirits, yes, not that the one implies the other. In most of the stories coming out of the South Bridge vaults and Greyfriars, no."

"But you write about such stories, even so."

"The tension between the world inside our heads and the world outside our heads defines our humanity."

After a moment's contemplation, Vasudev nodded approval. "You would be interested in *Commerce and Credibility*, then. It's a new book by Robin Davis from just here, Edinburgh University. So far as I understand it from the publicity material, he's attempting to prove that everything we consider supernatural is merely a construct of our own consciousness."

"Good luck to him. You can't prove ghosts and poltergeists and all exist any more than you can prove any sort of divine being exists. And you can't prove they don't." Jean jotted down the title even so. He was right. She was interested.

Chapter Six

"So how long have you owned the two buildings, then, Vasudev?" Miranda pulled the conversation out of suppositional quicksand and back to factual firm ground as smoothly as Alasdair would have done. Jean wrote "l", for "listen", and leaned back.

"Going on for three years now," answered Vasudev, "soon after I met Duncan over a game at St. Andrews. He told me there was good investment property near the South Bridge, especially since the fire of 2002. He was quite correct, very helpful of him. But there's been more than a spot of bother obtaining planning permission for the restaurant, the pub, the flats upstairs. We're still working on the flats in the Playfair Building. The ones at Lady Niddry's are finished and sold, bringing in a nice income."

"What about the shop on Lady Niddry's first floor?" asked Miranda.

Up the allegedly haunted staircase, Jean added to herself.

"Ah. Well now. That was a bit of a mis-judgment on my part. The clientele for an exclusive restaurant on the lower levels doesn't automatically transfer to an exclusive boutique upstairs. They're not open the same hours, for one thing. We've had to, ah . . ."

Miranda didn't say, *lower your sights*, but waited.

". . . change the direction of our marketing. We're well positioned for the city market, but also for the more casual university trade. Hence the pub in the Playfair Building."

"And there's always the tourist trade," murmured Miranda. "Not only the heritage industry, but the folk who are away from home and open to, ah, unusual shops."

"Quite so. We're hoping to be as versatile as possible."

An American would have said, cover all the bases. But

Jean wasn't sure about the equivalent British idiom. Guard both the wickets? She said, "I saw a woman standing in the window of the erotic gear shop, slender, long blond hair."

"That would be Nicola MacLaren, manageress."

Jean and Miranda caught each other's eyes in a simultaneous wince. "Manageress" was like Bewley's "female detective", implying males were the real thing, whether police inspectors or managers. Although Jean was uncomfortably aware that when it came to gender assumptions, today she was a pot dissing a kettle. "Is there really a Pippa somewhere behind the scenes, or did y'all decide that was simply a good name to class the place up?"

"Marketing," said Vasudev, with another shrug.

"A fine art," Miranda said.

"Our Nicola's a very versatile lady herself," Vasudev went on. "For one thing, she brought Des Bewley to our attention. They knew each other at university. She read business administration whilst he read English or the like, all very well but a subject that rarely leads to a real job."

"The like" could imply Jean's Ph.D. in History, although she'd once had a real job, as a professor of same, and was now gainfully employed in one of the few other jobs such a degree could have prepared her to do.

"He's worked in construction and the entertainment industry, is familiar with the local music scene. He's booked Hugh Munro and his band for the opening, and tells me he'll be choosing a wide variety of acts in the future—some for younger audiences, I'm sure, although Mr. Munro is, well . . ."

"A veteran of the scene," Jean suggested.

Nodding, Vasudev set his empty cup back on the tray. "We're converting the cellar into a stage, and now we may open up the vault below. After, of course, the present unpleasantness is resolved."

"As you did with Lady Niddry's Drawing Room?" asked Miranda. "I assume there was nothing, well, startling in those vaults?"

"We incorporated those vaults into our design, but they

were already open, Lady Niddry's being preceded by a casual student meeting place. I'm told that quite a few of the local musicians practiced in the South Bridge vaults, soon after they were opened in the early nineties. But I wasn't here then."

"Neither was I," Jean said, even as she added to herself, *but I know someone who was.*

"And I was neither a student nor a musician then," said Miranda. "Fancy that! Bands playing in those vaults! They were after deafening themselves, weren't they?"

Vasudev pulled out his phone, glanced at it, and shifted forward in his chair. "Time's getting on, ladies. If you'll excuse me . . ."

"Of course." Miranda stood up. "Just one last thing, Vasudev. Are you quite wedded to the name of the pub? The Resurrectionist?"

"Eh? What?" asked Vasudev as he, too, got to his feet.

"Can you imagine a tipsy chap after saying 'resurrectionist' to a taxi driver? Or anyone searching for it on-line, when the spelling's more than a bit tricky?"

"Ah. Good point, that."

"I was thinking 'Burke's Revenge'" Miranda went on.

"Burke? Of Burke and Hare?"

"Two of the Edinburgh tourist trade's favorite sons," said Jean. "Burke was the one that was hanged. Hare turned state's evidence. And Doctor Knox got off scot-free, if you'll pardon the expression"

"Queen's evidence," Miranda corrected.

"In the 1820s," corrected Jean back again, "it would be King's evidence."

"I'm sure it was." Miranda turned back to Vasudev. "I'm thinking you're on the right track—the Playfair Pub would be historically accurate, with William Playfair designing the South Bridge in . . ." She gestured toward Jean, who said, "1785." ". . . but would be hinting at a sporting association, with nothing of the South Bridge ambiance."

He was backing slowly toward the door. "I'll have a word with Bewley, shall I? See how he feels about the matter. Odds are, though, that the signage and all has already been ordered."

Miranda beamed on him. "Good to see you again. My regards to Sophie Marie and the children, eh?"

"Yes, yes, of course. Miss Fair—Jean, it was good to meet you at last."

"Nice to meet you, too."

Vasudev opened the door, walked into the hall, then turned back again, his hand pulling a leather wallet from his pocket. "Duncan happened to mention that you're recently married, Jean, and your husband is the head of Protect and Survive and a former detective as well. I hosted his predecessor a time or two at Lady Niddry's Drawing Room. Would you and he enjoy having a meal there as my guests? Tomorrow, if that's not too short a notice. The thirteenth, the night before St. Valentine's Day. We're having several friends of the management in that night. Cocktails at half past seven, a tasting menu at half past eight."

"Why thank you." Jean stepped forward to take the proffered business card.

"And of course, if you enjoyed your meal well enough to write about it in *Great Scot*, we'd greatly appreciate the mention."

"Thank you," Jean said again, while from the corner of her eye she saw Miranda's beam widen.

Vasudev turned left toward reception and his escape to the outer world. Just as Jean turned right toward her own office, her backpack emitted a tinny version of Burns' "My Love is Like a Red, Red, Rose", which, now that she thought about it, was appropriate for Valentine's Day even if it did mention June.

"It's himself, is it?" Miranda asked.

"Yep. Speak of the—well, he's neither a devil nor an angel, like most of us." Jean fished her phone from the bottom of the bag. "Hello, Alasdair."

"Hullo, Jean," said his voice in her ear.

She pitched her bag onto her desk and in two steps was across the tiny room and at the window. It was raining again, she saw. Umbrellas and raincoats swirled below her like debris in a stream, parting and re-joining around buses, cars, and taxis. Beyond the moss-edged slates of the rooftops, the clouds coagulated into swags and lumps, so that a watery sunlight gleamed between them and then faded. But not one face looked upward. "Any news?"

"I'm letting you know I escaped the dungeons is all," Alasdair replied. "I've paid my respects at the morgue and am on my way back to the office. Ian's looking out what plans of the area we've got."

The city morgue in all its fluorescent and Formica ambience might be an improvement over the catacombs, Jean told herself. It depended.

"Kazmarek's preparing post-mortems on both bodies," Alasdair went on. "He did notice one thing whilst they were packing up. Looks to be the man was hanged. Cervical bones broken in just the right pattern."

"A criminal? The medical school was only allowed to dissect the bodies of criminals, but there weren't enough . . . Well, we don't know that body snatchers have anything to do with either of them, do we?"

"Not one bit, no."

"And not everyone hanged in ye olden times was a criminal, not by today's standards," Jean said.

"Our ancestors could be an unforgiving lot."

Jean didn't dwell on that thought. "Miranda and I talked to Vasudev Prasad, the owner of both the Playfair Building and Lady Niddry's—along with Duncan, of course, although it sounds like Vasudev is the one making the day-to-day decisions. He says the manager of the pub, Des Bewley, told the plumbers to open up the closed door. Maybe because he heard Jason Pagano's in town."

"I was with you on the names until that last. Jason Pagano?"

"The TV host. 'Beyond the Edge'. Vampires, zombies, poltergeists, and assorted woo-woo, the louder the better. You remember, I was watching his show the other night."

"Ah. The one with the out-of-focus photos of a lass in a nightgown running about and screaming. And hearsay evidence rather than fact. A likely interview subject, you were thinking then, save his work's a bit dark for *Great Scot*."

"And he's English, too, but I won't hold that against him."

Somewhere within range of Alasdair's phone, a bus revved up and moved out. "Pagano's looking out material here in Auld Reekie, is he?"

"Apparently so. All the usual, plus Vasudev says a waiter saw a ghost, gender unspecified, fall from the main staircase at Lady Niddry's. Fall, or jumped, or was pushed . . . Well, that's no more than hearsay of hearsay, really, but you never know what's important, even in a cold case."

"Aye, that's so."

"Didn't Knox say she was talking to the plumbers and Bewley today? And Amy Herries, too. What do you remember of her sister's disappearance?"

"Very little. University student, liked a late night with the lasses—and the lads as well. Here's everyone assuming 'til now she was away with the boyfriend. Knox is telling me he was American like you."

Jean leaned back against the edge of her desk. "And now the boyfriend's a person of interest, right?"

"Right. A bit late to be picking up his trail, but there you are."

"There's someone else Knox needs to talk to. Nicola MacLaren, the manager of the shop on the second, er, first floor of Lady Niddry's. Did you happen to notice it as you walked by—'Pippa's Erotic Gear'?"

"I was by way of taking note, oh aye," Alasdair said.

"Nicola recommended Bewley for the job at the pub. The cop on duty outside the door told me he saw them not just together this morning, he saw Nicola bawling Bewley out."

"Hearsay . . ."

"Vasudev said she was versatile—I don't know, maybe she has a side job as a dominatrix and Bewley's a customer. She was wearing a vinyl outfit when I saw her looking out of the window."

"Never knowing what's important? Or are you having a moment of prurient interest?"

She had to puzzle a moment over the last two words—the three rolled *r's* were a bit much even for her Scot-adapted ears. Then she laughed. "Of course I am. However, it's Lady Niddry's Drawing Room we'll be seeing tomorrow, not the shop upstairs. Vasudev's invited us for a free Valentine's dinner."

"Has he, now? Wanting a good review, I reckon."

"Of course. All bow down to the great god marketing, home address the corner of Mammon and Crassus. You know, crass?"

She could hear the *yes dear* in his chuckle, but he said only. "Friday the thirteenth. Sounds to be the perfect evening for a romantic dinner in the South Bridge vaults."

"Well, supposedly it's only sort of in the vaults . . . Whatever. Right now I'm going to call Michael at the Museum and see what he knows about the vaults back when they were first opened up. Vasudev says music groups used to practice there, and Michael was in a group when he was a student at the university."

"There were pipe bands practicing in the vaults?"

"That was before he was in the pipe band, when he was doing folk-rock stuff. Rebecca was talking about it on Saturday, remember? When she told Hugh it's a shame he and Michael never caught up with each other until I introduced them last year?"

This time Alasdair actually uttered his equivalent of *yes dear:* "Oh aye, lass, anything you say."

She suspected she did get the eye-roll this time. Responding in kind, she turned her eyes to the window just in time to see a ray of sun split the clouds like the fiery sword of judgment and then vanish again.

"It's time I was getting to work," she said. "With any luck, the sun will make an appearance this afternoon, remind us what light is."

"Just saw a positively brilliant beam." Behind Alasdair's reply, a door opened. "I've arrived—time for me to be working as well. Later, Jean."

"Righty-ho," she said, channeling Miranda, and ended the call.

There was the sun again, now you see it, now you don't. Dark, light, dark . . . And what had been the last thing the woman in the vault had seen? Had she gone to the light or to the darkness?

Turning her back, however briefly, on the window, Jean both switched on her computer and found Michael Campbell-Reid's name on the menu of her phone.

Chapter Seven

Jean buttoned up her coat, threw her backpack over her shoulder, and pulled open the outside door. "Good night, Gavin."

His head popped up like a prairie dog's—oh, he was wrestling with a power strip beneath his desk. "You're leaving early to make up for coming in late, are you now?"

"I ate lunch at my desk," Jean returned in mock indignation. "Besides, I'm on the trail of a new article, even though right now it's just one of those weird and disturbing stories."

"Oh aye, it is that . . . Jings!" The lights flickered and he dived back to his task.

Smiling, Jean retreated down the turnpike stair and through the outside door, where a gust of cold wind made her pull up her hood. At least the wind was shredding the rain clouds. Low above the southwestern rooftops, the sun threw streaks of light and shadow across the street and then snatched them away.

Any other winter day she wouldn't have minded that quitting time coincided with sunset. After all, she lived amid multiple modern conveniences—even if picturesque old buildings and modern conveniences such as electricity didn't always play nicely together. This evening, though, she had an appointment in what some ghostmongers called the most haunted churchyard in the world.

She scurried along the teeming sidewalks past more than a few buildings displaying a P&S shield, a gold griffin on a field of red, and across the George IV Bridge, which spanned the Cowgate to the west of the South Bridge. It had its share of nightclubs and bars, but not nearly as many spooky stories, go figure.

Passing the dashing new Museum of Scotland, a medieval fortress re-imagined for the twenty-first century, Jean hurried across Candlemaker Row and into the dark, musty groove between two older buildings. At the far end, a tall figure waited beneath the wrought-iron arch reading "Grey" and "Friars". "Jean! Hullo!"

"Hey, Michael," Jean said. "I would have been glad to meet you in the Museum."

"I'm away early the day, meeting Rebecca at the far gate. She's got tickets for a concert at St. Cuthbert's. Good job the wean likes music—she'll sleep right through, I reckon."

"Little Linda inherited her musical ear from you. In fact, it's music I wanted to ask you about. To begin with, at least." Side by side they stepped through the gateway into Greyfriars Kirkyard.

High walls and higher buildings enclosed the open area with its leaf-strewn grass and naked trees. Many of the windows overlooking the cemetery and church were guarded by iron bars, as though either iron or bars would keep out wandering spirits, be they benign, malicious, or merely bewildered. The weather-darkened tombs lining the walls and dimpling the turf were carved in a style that Jean thought of as exuberant mortality, skulls, bones, and effigies filling the niches between columns and beneath pediments. Even the legend of Greyfriars Bobby, about the simple loyalty of a dog, hardly lightened the atmosphere. And yet Greyfriars Kirkyard served as a park in the heart of the city. Office workers ate their lunches here, and on summer days people sunbathed on the lawn.

Jekyll and Hyde, Jean told herself. *Written by Edinburgh native Robert Louis Stevenson. Who also wrote about body snatchers.*

Michael wasn't taking in the entire scene, but only a part of it—the film crew blocking the sidewalk in front of the far gate. "There's the other reason I was after meeting you in the kirkyard." he said. "That lot was in the Museum earlier, looking out torture devices. You'll find them amusing, I reckon. The folk, not the thumbscrews and such like."

Sunlight flared. The long, raking shadows darkened even

as the yellow stucco sides of Greyfriars Kirk glowed. A gaggle of spectators eddied and parted, revealing a broad-shouldered man with black hair, black goatee, black leather jacket and black boots, the piratical effect only mitigated by the dark glasses hanging from the neck of his black T-shirt.

Speak of the devil. Jean said, "That's Jason Pagano."

"The chap with 'Beyond the Edge', oh aye. Horror rather than history. Either way, he's spoilt for choice here in Edinburgh." Michael and Jean drifted closer to scene of the action.

Pagano took up a wide-legged stance in front of the camera, next to a woman whose wilted trench coat and name badge declared her a local guide as much as her accent did. "Twas Mary, Queen of Scots," she said, "who ordered the opening of Greyfriars, as too many folk had been buried round St. Giles and the cemetery was heaving."

"Have there been any reports of Mary haunting Greyfriars?" Pagano asked in a deep, resonant voice, his own accent hovering somewhere over the mid-Atlantic.

"Ach, no, she's walking hereabouts, make no mistake—she's been seen at Holyrood, at the foot of the Royal Mile—but Greyfriars has its own specters, none so harmless as Mary."

"The evil walking these grounds came later," Pagano said to the camera, and the trill of a cell phone broke the hush.

"Sorry." The guide dived toward a handbag perched on a nearby gravestone.

The camera man stood down. Scowling, Pagano extracted a couple of note cards from his pocket and said, not at all to himself, "A group of Scottish Puritans signed a contract or covenant here soon after Mary's death."

"Not all that soon. Mary died in 1587. The Covenant was signed in 1638." Jean had intended her voice to carry only to Michael—his field was the thirteenth century, not the seventeenth—but some caprice of the wind carried it to Pagano's ears.

He jerked around, his scowl sweeping the watching faces.

Jean raised her hand. "Hi. Historian here."

"And here," added Michael, perhaps out of chivalry, perhaps simply to set the record straight.

Just as Pagano's oddly pale eyes beneath their heavy brows focused on them both, a man wearing a black windbreaker—Jean sensed a theme—and holding a tablet computer stepped forward. "Jason, this light's the best we've had all day, and it won't last long. We need to get going with Liz and the re-enactment. Besides, it'd be better to talk to the guide in front of a creepy tomb, not the church. There's one down that way that way that looks like a nightmare."

"And we're running late why, Ryan?" Pagano's words were soft, but his tone had a chip on its shoulder. No wonder. Ryan, with his face puckered around glasses, his carrot-colored mop of hair, and his slight build, looked like the sort of guy that guys like Pagano would dunk in the toilet.

"Sorry, sorry," said Ryan. "I was delayed, traffic, couldn't help it . . ."

Turning his back on Ryan, to say nothing of Jean, Michael, and the other kibitzers, Pagano strode to where a young woman, Liz, presumably, was adjusting her bonnet, wide collar, and long skirt. Seventeenth-century clothing, Jean noted. Like that worn by the ghost in the vault beneath the Playfair Building.

The entire company, cameras, guide, re-enactor and all, surged toward the far corner of the Kirkyard, followed by the scrum of onlookers. There Pagano resumed his stance on the steps of a cylindrical mausoleum, his shoulder against the iron grille covering its doorway. Liz strolled on through another gateway, its iron grille open onto a long narrow space lined with yet more mausoleums, empty doorway after doorway turned toward each other like two ranks of blind soldiers.

"Go for it!" called Ryan.

The lights from the camera glared out, whiter and brighter than the sunlight, and shadows flickered in the interior behind the black leather shoulders. Jean thought of the glare of the police lamps in the vault. But that wasn't even a pauper's grave. It was no grave at all. This, however, was the burial place of a rich and powerful man, George MacKenzie, Lord Advocate of Scotland.

"The Covenanters wanted to run their churches without any interference from the king. In 1679, Government troops chased them down and imprisoned them in this corner of Greyfriars Kirkyard. Those who didn't die of exposure were tortured and murdered by George Mackenzie, the judge buried here—whoa! What's that?" Pagano jerked away from the grille and spun around. "Something grabbed at me!"

His motion was so sudden Jean's heart bumped upwards, and beside her Michael twitched. But it was all part of the show. Nothing moved beyond the grille but the shadows generated by Pagano's own crew.

He turned back around and lowered his voice, so that the sibilants hissed. "It was only a few years ago a homeless man broke into this tomb, looking for a place to sleep. Whatever he saw here, whatever happened to him here, drove him mad." With a knowing look directly into the camera, Pagano paced toward the gateway. "This gate is usually kept locked. Bad things happen to people here after dark. But we have special permission to go inside."

A flashbulb went off amidst the kibitzers.

"Hold it!" Ryan yelled, and rounded on a gray-haired square-jawed man still holding a camera before his face. "Please, sir, no photos."

"No photos," Pagano repeated, pointedly leaving off the courtesies.

The man waved a hand, less in apology than in dismissal, and melted back into the gathered bodies.

"Any tour group can get special permission," Jean said. "Although why anyone would want to go in there after dark, I don't know. All part of the Edinburgh experience, I guess."

The wind blew Michael's reddish-brown hair back from his brow. His blue eyes, still focused on Pagano, sparked with intelligent skepticism. "That was a potted history of a potted history for you."

"No kidding. Scholars have trouble keeping it all straight,

let alone TV hosts. You've got Knox and the Reformation, you've got Presbyterians against the Catholics and the Episcopal Church, you've got the royalists against the Covenanters, the highlanders against the lowlanders, the English parliamentarians, the Restoration, civil war upon civil war, faith versus public order, Covenanters holding services in open air rather than in government-sanctioned churches. And more than enough cruelty to go around."

"Some of the royalists were exhuming the bodies of dead Covenanting leaders and dismembering or beheading them."

"Alasdair was just saying that our ancestors were an unforgiving lot." Jean thought of the second body in the vault, hanged and disarticulated.

Michael nodded. "Too many folk today would be as vindictive, given the chance."

"Yeah." Not that the first body, the woman's, had any obvious injuries.

Since the circus had rolled away from the sidewalk beside the church, Michael and Jean headed toward the back gate and his rendezvous. They skirted several extension cords snaking across the grass, Jean thinking that George Mackenzie would have found electricity to be a handy-dandy torture device.

She paused next to the two mortsafes tucked side by side into the lawn. "To leap from the seventeenth century to the nineteenth century, I saw a mortsafe earlier today, in one of the South Bridge vaults."

"Did you now? Is it in good enough condition to display in the Museum?"

"I don't know. It's pretty rusty. It's in better condition than the two bodies in the same chamber, though."

Michael looked down at her. "Eh?"

She told him the tale, including her suggestion about sending the decayed book to the Museum, and concluded, "The man was hanged, apparently, and it looked like he had a Bible with him, and since the ghost is dressed pretty much like Liz there . . ."

The cameras swiveled, Ryan gestured, and Liz came

running out of the gateway, cap askew, large dark eyes bulging, mouth open on a scream which reverberated eerily in the stone-lined enclosure—the sarcophagus—of the kirkyard.

Michael glanced at Jean, brows reaching for the sky. Jean shrugged. By the time that sequence was broadcast, both Liz and her setting would be computerized into a soft-focus slo-mo twilight.

Pagano turned to the camera and said, "Something evil lurks in the Covenanter's Prison, biting and scratching visitors. But it can't be contained by stone walls and iron bars. Is it the demented spirit of George Mackenzie, released by the intruder? Does the Mackenzie Poltergeist also roam the South Bridge vaults? When we come back, we'll find out."

"Great!" shouted Ryan. "We got it!"

"So he is planning a show in the vaults," Jean said, mostly to herself. "I won't be swooning in surprise at that."

Chapter Eight

"No ghostmonger'll be missing out the vaults." Michael considered the mortsafes, his head tilted to the side. "You're thinking the man in the vault might be a Covenanter? But the South Bridge vaults were built . . ."

"A hundred years later. Yeah, I know. There's just as much logic in my connecting the body to the Covenanters as in ghostmongers like Jason Pagano saying the Mackenzie Poltergeist roams the vaults. In the seventeenth century there were no vaults, only the Cowgate meandering along the valley paralleling the High Street."

"Are ghosts logical, then? Is a poltergeist by way of being a ghost, and not some sort of weird phenomenon?"

"Are people being scratched at all? Usually poltergeists move things and throw them around. Assuming poltergeists actually exist."

"Well, some folk would question the existence of ghosts, or of emotional resonances caught in physical objects, but . . ."

"But," Jean concluded. "Oops, we'd better move on."

The film crew started back toward the church and Jean and Michael moved on, but not before Pagano shot them another piercing look. Jean bared every tooth and a couple of fillings in a smile. "Thanks! Good show!"

A young woman wearing a denim mini-skirt and a scanty version of Pagano's black leather jacket sidled up to him and extended a notebook. "Jason, would you mind signing my wee book?"

Pagano made an about-face toward her. "My pleasure. And what's your name?"

In private, Jean noted, the TV host's accent gravitated to the English Midlands. Of course he'd adopt a more neutral accent to sell his show in the US. Ryan, now—his accent was neither mid-Atlantic nor Midlands, it was Midwestern U.S. Jean could hear the cornfields and the catfish. Liz sounded English, although the long black hair tumbling down as she removed her cap might indicate some cross-Channel ancestry.

What color had Sara's hair been? Had she been a good Scots—or mid-American—redhead? Had she been darker in coloring, like Pagano? Jean couldn't remember what Amy Herries looked like. The encounter had been too brief, leaving her with only an image of smeared eyeliner and a wail of grief and resentment.

"Even if the woman is Sara Herries," she said to Michael, "how did she get into a closed-off vault back in the mid-nineties? A question that leads me to you, of course. You were at the university then."

"And my band was practicing in the vaults."

"Not the one beneath the Playfair Building, I assume."

"Had no clue that was there, no."

"Vasudev Prasad, the guy who owns the property, was saying Lady Niddry's used to be a student hang-out."

"Oh aye. Beer, crisps, music, raves—we were calling it 'The Body Snatcher', just for a bit of fun."

Jean grinned, thinking of her "Body Snatchers Are Us" comment to Miranda. "Fun being relative."

"Especially at that age. We were making too much noise to be scared by ghosts or tattie bogles or body snatchers, I'm telling you that. It wasn't only our lads, either. Some nights several groups'd be playing in different areas. There was no one charging us for the space—no one had thought yet to develop the vaults. They were just empty rooms, more than a little uncanny, oh aye, and the acoustics weren't the best, but when you're a student, 'no charge' decides the matter."

"Several groups playing at once? And you with bagpipes? It must have been deafening."

"My ears are ringing still," Michael said with a grimace. "Mind you, it's Hugh you should be asking. I've only ever been a hobbyist."

"It's possible Sara was a musician or a groupie, but even if she was, that doesn't explain . . ." Jean sighed. "So do you remember the Sara Herries case? She disappeared from a pub on the South Bridge in 1996."

"I'm remembering, oh aye. My first brush with crime, if at quite a remove—I had an undergraduate class with her is all, the year before she went missing. She was considering reading history, same as me, though I ended by deciding on history and archaeology and she changed her mind, went elsewhere. Far as I'm remembering, she was a bit of a Goth, likely would have been a fan of yon Pagano. But I canna say any more about her than that. I never had anything to help the police with their inquiries. Less couthy polis than Alasdair, mind, but then, they were hardly making social calls."

"They rarely are, more's the pity," Jean said.

The sun dipped below the roofs and shadow thickened in the kirkyard. Any warmth the sunshine had held—more psychological than real—ebbed into coolth. The traffic noise from beyond the walls seemed muted, held by a barrier not of space but of time. Except for the sound of sirens going by, first a police car, Jean decided, followed a moment late by an ambulance.

Michael bent to peer into an empty mausoleum, the sculptured skulls protruding from its doorway partly chipped away, partly fouled not just with bird droppings but with what looked like blood but had to be ketchup. In the gloomy interior of the tomb, cellophane snack bags rustled in a chill draft. "The same sad folk are out and about here of a night that once lived in the vaults. The poor, the muddled, the criminals who prey on them."

"And the ghostmongers. Better than body-snatchers, I guess. Brain-snatchers. Pretend danger, not the genuine article. History interpretation, ditto." Jean glanced back at Pagano and his crew, now packing up. Or the crew was packing up, rather, while Pagano stood aside, one hand holding a phone against his ear, the other chopping the air.

She and Michael ducked into a passage between two rows of yet more mausoleums. The gateway at the end opened onto a wide lawn surrounding a turreted building seemingly teleported in from Ruritania.

"Robin Davis," Michael said suddenly. "I don't know him, myself, but I'm thinking Sara was working for him as a research assistant. He's a bit of a goat with the undergraduate lasses, mind you, or was at the time. Had his favorites. But I reckon the polis had a word or two, eh?"

"Robin Davis?" repeated Jean. "Vasudev was just talking about his new book. *Commerce* and something . . ."

"*Commerce and Credibility*, oh aye. He's saying that people are much more likely to have supernatural experiences in the vaults or here in the Kirkyard or at Mary King's Close, any site rumored to be haunted, if they go there expecting something supernatural to happen."

"That's psychology more than history, although history is all about people and their psychology."

"Davis is doing social anthropology, right enough."

"And Sara was researching for him? That doesn't tie in with her being a fan of Pagano—well, I'm building bricks without clay, let alone without straw."

"That you are."

A woman pushing a stroller appeared in the far gateway and waved. Michael and Jean waved back.

"Seeing is believing, and believing is seeing," Jean said. "That's my working thesis in a nutshell."

"Davis's working thesis goes further. He's saying it's all belief and no seeing. He's even implying in his conclusion that religion is just as false as ghosts and other paranormal beasties."

"There's an implication that would have led to some pretty grim repercussions in past times, which is more than a few ghost stories have ever done. Unless you're thinking of father, son, and holy ghost. Vasudev was asking whether a ghost had to be Christian in order to be deterred by a cross."

"Shows the cultural implications of the supernatural, Davis'd be saying."

"True. But it's religion that's a very complex matter of culture and politics as much as faith, while ghosts—just happen."

"To some folk," Michael told her with a grin, and raised his voice. "Hullo there!"

Rebecca maneuvered the stroller down the walk, between ranks of doorways both blank and bricked, between palisades of memorial plaques and other intimations of mortality. Enclosed by a plastic weather-proof bubble and layers of knit garments, little Linda looked like a hothouse orchid, if orchids had bright eyes and rosy cheeks. Cheerfully oblivious to her surroundings, she shouted, "Da-da!"

"There's my lass." Michael tweaked a lock of auburn hair that escaped Linda's Fair Isle-patterned cap.

Rebecca wore a knit cap that matched her daughter's. Its bobble bobbed as she turned to Jean, her brown eyes sparking with curiosity. "Are you on the trail of a story, Jean, or on another case?"

"Story," Jean replied, just as Michael answered, "Case."

"Both," admitted Jean. "Alasdair's got an official toe in the door and I'm playing professional nosy parker. This one's more of an academic exercise than an immediate threat to—to our life and limbs, anyway," she concluded, wondering if that sounded quite as cold-hearted as it felt.

"Anything to do with that mob?" Rebecca looked past them at the work party in the kirkyard. "Whoa. Who's the metrosexual Rasputin?"

Michael guffawed. Jean whooped. The sound, channeled by the avenue of stone, turned several heads, including Pagano's razor-cut and heavily gelled one.

Jean answered, "That's someone who wishes we'd shut up and go away. Jason Pagano, 'Beyond the Edge'."

"One of those supernatural TV shows, right?" Rebecca replied.

"His guide was telling him that the ghost of Mary walks at Holyrood. Neither Alasdair nor I have ever picked up anything there, though."

"I get the occasional quiver from handling her things, and I may have heard a few footsteps and the like. But then, I may be expecting to hear footsteps."

"And there we are," Michael said, as though some issue had been settled. He took the handles of the stroller and turned it back toward the gate. "We're away, then. Are you going home, Jean?"

"Yeah, but . . ." She could have walked with them, and reached Ramsay Garden via the West Bow, but the Cowgate lay behind her. "Not tonight. Y'all enjoy the concert."

"We will, thank you," said Rebecca, and took Michael's arm.

"If I'm remembering anything about the Herries case, I'll be giving you a shout, eh?" Michael said over his shoulder.

"Who?" Rebecca asked.

"The game's afoot," Michael told her. "Alasdair's on the case. Our tale began this morning in the South Bridge vaults . . ."

"Good night!" Jean called after them. She strolled back into the kirkyard, skirting the television crew. In the dusk they were fast devolving into dim shapes illuminated only by the occasional small comet of a flashlight or the red, pungent tip of a cigarette.

Pagano's voice said in the gloom, "Of course I'd be interested in a contemporary murder. A university student, you're saying? Proof of evil presences in the vaults, that will do nicely. Ta."

What? Who said anything about murder? She looked around so quickly her neck almost snapped, but couldn't distinguish him from the others, let alone see who he was talking to, in person or on his phone. Her foot slipped off the side of the walk, her ankle twisted, and it was only with an ungainly flail and lurch that she kept herself from falling onto the mortsafes. Which would have done neither antique iron bars nor living flesh any good.

A hand seized her forearm. A breathless voice demanded, "You all right, ma'am?"

She looked around to see Ryan's pale face barely a foot from her own, his eyes so wide the whites glinted. Good grief, had she looked that much like a train wreck? She tested her ankle. *Whew. A-okay.* "I'm fine, thanks."

"No problem." Releasing her, Ryan spun back around to the group. There was Pagano, a hulking black presence in the darkness, just tucking something—his phone?—into his pocket. So who had called him? A handler who'd read the morning paper? Whoever it was who'd tipped him off about the ghost at Lady Niddry's?

It was about time she touched bases or knocked wickets or whatever with Alasdair. Funny, how she used to be a complete brain all by herself.

This time watching where she was going, Jean walked on wondering if there were indeed any ghosts or spirits or uncanny presences in Greyfriars Kirkyard. Despite its reputation, she'd never sensed anything there other than sorrow, and that was probably the grief of the survivors. It wasn't the most peaceful of cemeteries, but still, it was populated only with the surrendered husks of humanity. Any lingering memory-images gathered elsewhere.

Once through the passage onto Candlemaker Row, she paused beneath a streetlight, inhaled the scent of frying food emanating from the pub on the corner, and considered the mouth of the Cowgate a block or so away. Tempted as she was to walk along it, there was no point. It wasn't as though she had x-ray vision, and would be able to see through the massed buildings below and beside the South Bridge to the newly opened and unfortunately inhabited vault. Still, it never hurt to try a different perspective. Maybe tomorrow, in whatever sunlight the day served up.

Headlights raked the front of the Museum and her mini-backpack trilled of roses and June. She dived into her bag—Murphy's Physics, the item she wanted was always at the bottom—and came up with her phone. "Hey, Alasdair."

"Where are you, Jean? Still with Michael at the Museum?"

"Yes and no. We actually met at Greyfriars, but I'm standing outside the Museum right now. Why?"

"Come back by the South Bridge, then. The cop watching

the Playfair Building's gone down the stairs onto his head."

What? That would explain the sirens. Her feet already carrying her across the street, she said, "Oh no. What a place for an accident."

"Accident? Not a bit of it. He looks to have been coshed by a handy hammer and pushed."

Coshed. Pushed. "I'm on my way," she said, and broke into a run.

Chapter Nine

It was *déjà vu* all over again, except in artificial light. This time the police car outside the door was supplemented by another one and by an ambulance, its back doors gaping open. The glow spilling from the interior illuminated a circle of watching faces, including that of Sergeant Gordon. He was barring the door, his height intimidating even if his body build was not. Jean would have called him cadaverous if she hadn't first met him in the company of two cadavers.

Which was something she hoped the coshed constable was not. She pushed through the crowd and said to Gordon between breaths, "It's Jean Fairbairn. Alasdair called me . . ."

"Inside," he said, without stepping out of the way.

She squeezed past and into the paint scent of the hallway. Men were still at work inside the bar, and Des Bewley stood in the doorway, hard hat balanced atop his head, as though he hadn't budged all day. "You again," he said, on yet a stronger waft of alcohol.

"Yeah, me again. What's going on?"

"They all packed up and left, without that red-headed Amazon giving me the time of day, mind you, and moved that chap from the street door to the old door in the cellar. There he's sitting, the hours passing, and here's me taking pity on him and handing over a bag of crisps and an Irn-Bru, gratis."

Irn-Bru tasted like liquid bubblegum to Jean, but no matter, not now.

"Then he's gone," Bewley went on, "and his mates come looking for him, and he turns up in the vault."

"Not the cellar? The vault itself?"

"My lot's working in the cellar, aren't they? Coming and going, up and down. And the dustmen here as well, making a start on shifting the rubbish." Bewley's already full bottom lip sagged into something between resentment and a pout. "Didn't see a thing, Madam detective-bloody-Knox to the contrary."

"Jean?" Alasdair looked out of the entrance to the stairwell. "This way."

"Thank you," Jean told Bewley. A few steps, and she asked Alasdair, "Is he all right? Rudolph, I mean—I can tell Bewley's okay . . ."

"Rudolph?"

Oh. She fluttered a hand. *Never mind.* "The constable. The same one who was at the door when we were here this morning, right? I talked to him—he pointed out Nicola MacLaren and Bewley and everything."

"Concussion," answered Alasdair, "and likely bumps and bruises to spare, but he's partly conscious and moving about."

"That's good." Jean exhaled a sigh of relief. "No chance of asking him what happened, I guess."

"Not yet. Ah . . ." He stepped aside, pulling Jean with him, as a procession came up the stairs. Paramedics maneuvered a stretcher with the poor red-nosed constable now a sickly chalk-white beneath his bandages. Knox, doing her best Medusa impersonation, brought up the rear. She moderated her scowl into a curt nod at Jean, ignored Bewley, and brushed Gordon aside. Flashes of light outside were no doubt the cameras of Jean's step-brethren in the Fourth Estate.

She found herself huddled with Alasdair in a corner of the hall, beside a couple of crates stamped "Glassware Made in China". He indicated the folder of papers in his hand. "The call was coming in just as I arrived at police headquarters with the few plans Ian and I turned up, and Knox was after bringing me here along with her."

"You could have left the folder at her office."

"I did do. This one's ours, for what good it'll do. Apart from copies of a few original sketches, almost all the references we've got refer to the buildings destroyed in the fire, further along the South Bridge. These vaults here, they don't exist, not according to any schematics belonging to Protect and Survive."

"Well, they didn't just pop out of the space-time

continuum," said Jean, and, as Knox stepped back into the hallway, "She's being really accommodating, letting you into the case."

"Save I'm not asking her to. I'm retired."

"Sure you are," Jean murmured.

He opened his mouth, apparently thought better of speaking, and contented himself with a short, sharp snort. "I'm not sure what she's on about. Using me to ginger Gordon up, like as not."

Gordon followed Knox inside, pulling a notebook from his pocket. They bracketed Bewley. "What happened here?" Knox demanded.

To the accompaniment of power saws and nail guns, Bewley more or less repeated the sequence he'd related to Jean, leaving out the bit about the red-headed Amazon, elaborating on his kindness in not only giving Rudolph chips and Irn-Bru but also allowing Edinburgh's finest access to his loo.

"I even had an eye to the door whilst he was there," Bewley concluded. "None of my workmen saw him go down the cellar, never mind down the vault. Folk were coming and going all the day, not a soul not supposed to be here, not so's I could be telling, at the least. Who's going to . . ."

Notice one constable, Jean finished for him, *who wasn't missed until he went missing.*

"Has anything been taken from the cellar?" asked Gordon, while Knox shifted her weight and crossed her arms.

"Damned if I know. There's still rubbish wants throwing out. Could be Lady Niddry's silver tea set's hidden away there, eh?" Bewley rolled his eyes from sergeant to inspector and back, but got no reaction. He went on, "What of the vault? You lot were making photos and such. Anything missing from there?"

"We don't think so, no," answered Knox, even as Gordon muttered something about fresh footprints, now that the paramedics had trodden on the lot.

"Hm," Alasdair said in Jean's ear. "I walked from one dead end to the other with him this morning, should be only our own prints. But stone floors don't take footprints, just the wet patches."

"You wouldn't think a deteriorating mortsafe would attract a thief," she replied. "Maybe a reporter, but a reporter wouldn't bash a policeman. Not for a story like this, anyway."

"We had your plumbers in," Knox was telling Bewley. "You told them to open the blocked door and even lent a hand with the chisel. That's not what you said earlier, is it now?"

Bewley ducked his head, coiled his shoulders, and squirmed. "Have you ever gone jumping through hoops getting planning permission for an historic building?"

Yes, thought Jean.

"No," Gordon said. "Bending the law a bit, were you?"

"A plumber in Edinburgh could moonlight as an archaeologist," said Knox. "Just digging a hole is fraught with complications. Either you have the proper council bureaucrats on speed-dial, or you hide your discoveries before you forfeit your planning permissions. Is that it, Bewley?"

A mutter emanated from beneath the brim of Bewley's hat. "What?"

"Aye, I was telling them to open the door. There's vaults across the street, there's vaults next door, there had to be vaults here, ones we could be using to attract trade, eh? No harm in attracting trade. Edinburgh Council spends millions of quid attracting trade. But here's me, attracting the polis. It's not my fault there's nasties in the dungeons instead of silver tea sets." He glared from face to face.

Gordon glared back. Knox's hazel eyes considered Bewley like a specimen under glass labeled: *Person of interest. Not helpful.*

Jean felt a stirring of pity for him. Here was a man suffering from buyer's remorse. If only he'd left well enough alone. But it wasn't in human nature to do that. At least he wouldn't be in trouble with Vasudev Prasad—who had so smoothly confessed to calling *The Scotsman* this morning, as well as to agreeing with Bewley's initiative, before he could be caught out.

Knox turned away. Gordon pocketed his notebook.

Bewley jammed his hat even further onto his head, as though corking a bottle under pressure, and his body inclined toward the door of the bar. Jean stepped forward. "Mr. Bewley. Did you call Jason Pagano and tell him about the, ah, nasties in the dungeons?"

Three faces swung toward her. Four, counting Alasdair's— she could sense his scrutiny like an electrical field prickling on her temple.

"Who?" asked Gordon.

"Television chap," Knox said. "Presents one of those tatty ghost-hunting programs."

Bewley stared, jowls working.

"Answer the question," Gordon ordered him.

"No, I didn't go calling a presenter from the telly," Bewley snapped, and, after a deep intake of breath, "How'd I be knowing the man's phone number, eh? He's a celebrity. I'm a poor sod after doing honest work. Which needs doing."

"Get to it, then," said Knox, and Bewley made his escape into the bar.

"The man's an idiot," Gordon said, "either thinking we'll believe he saw nowt, or seeing nowt when he's been on the spot all day."

"Loads of people coming and going," Alasdair murmured.

Knox told Gordon, "You as well. Get to it. Start asking the workmen what they heard or saw. Who was where and when. And when you're finished with the workmen in this building, try the people in the area, next door, across the street."

"Like Nicola MacLaren across the street," Jean told them. "She manages Pippa's Erotic Gear, above Lady Niddry's."

Alasdair added, "She was seen ticking off Bewley this morning."

That's another seemingly backwards expression, Jean told herself. Here, to tick someone off meant to berate them, not to make them angry. "She was seen by the constable who just ended up at the bottom of the stairs."

"No reason to go assuming that's more than coincidence,"

cautioned Alasdair.

"P.C. Ross was telling me as well, when I left the scene this morning. The lad's either observant or imaginative." Knox looked from Alasdair's face to Jean's and back again without asking them to choose one, and turned to Gordon. "Carry on."

For a long count of three the inspector and her sergeant exchanged not glares, but looks of calculation. Then Gordon spun around and clattered down the stairs.

Knox turned back to Jean, but Alasdair was there first. "Someone was phoning Pagano about the bodies in the vault?"

"I just saw him with his crew in Greyfriars Kirkyard, taping an episode. Or part of one, anyway. I heard him talking, I think on his phone, saying something like, 'Of course I'm interested in a contemporary murder. A university student? Proof of an evil presence in the vaults, that will do nicely. Thanks.' Except I bet he said 'Ta'. I turned my ankle right then and didn't quite hear."

"Your ankle?" Alasdair glanced down at the bit of anatomy in question.

"It's fine. I caught myself, and Ryan, Pagano's director or whatever, grabbed me. I'm more likely to have a bruise on my arm from his grip than any kind of sprain."

Knox's brows knotted over the bridge of her nose. "He said 'university student'? Someone told him the body is Sara Herries before we announced it to the press?"

"It is Sara, then?" Alasdair asked.

"Dental records. Cut, dried, and fast. It's her all right."

"Cause of death?"

"Looks to be a blow to the head, Kazmarek is saying."

"A malicious blow, or the sort of injury happening in a fall down the stairs?"

Knox shook her head. "The wound's sharp-edged, but with the decay—well, he's having a closer look."

The sort of blow that had felled Constable Rudolph, Jean thought. "It's murder, then."

"Likely so, yes."

Rather than letting the word "murder" fester in the

darkened hallway, to say nothing of the knowledge that the murderer was apparently still keeping an eye on the place, Jean plunged on. "Did I notice some gold jewelry on her body?"

"A fine gold chain. Looks to have fallen into her blouse when the clasp broke. The pendant was lying beneath her, a wee gold Celtic cross."

"What if she was mugged, and the mugger grabbed the necklace, which broke it, and . . ."

"She was having a wander through the vault when she was mugged?" asked Alasdair.

"Yeah, well," Jean conceded.

"Well then," he went on, "someone's telling Pagano she was murdered when Dr. Kazmarek's just now ruling on the cause of death. Unless that someone's meaning the older body."

"Chance would be a fine thing," Knox replied sarcastically. "I'm not sure it's worth having Pagano in for questioning just now, though."

Jean conceded again, "It's hearsay. I understand."

Alasdair looked up at Knox, his stance not at all intimidated by her height, and said, "You were speaking to Amy Herries just as the balloon went up here, weren't you now? I saw the pair of you standing in the hall."

"Yes. I told her we'd identified the body as her sister's and asked her what she knew about the disappearance. Precious little, as it turned out. Not at all cooperative. At least she's stopped blubbing."

Jean didn't point out to Knox that, as it turned out, Amy hadn't been jumping to conclusions at all. As for being helpful, she was probably in shock. Or resentful.

"Inspector," called a constable from the cellar door, and without another word Knox smoothed the spikes of her hair— they sprang right back up again—and marched off to join her colleagues downstairs.

Alasdair turned his gaze on Jean. She turned her gaze on him. "The chap's looking for proof of evil presences in the vaults, then," he said. "There's a word used gey loosely. Proof."

"We've heard that one before. The proof's in the pudding. The exception that proves the rule. Ninety-proof spirits, to get back round to Miranda and her whisky connection."

"Hearsay," Alasdair stated.

"I know what I heard . . ."

"Oh aye, I'm not faulting you, I reckon your ears perked up like Dougie's at the can opener."

Jean smiled at that simile. ". . . but it's like seeing the ghost there in the vault. Without independent confirmation . . ."

"Right. Shall we?" Alasdair escorted her to the door and through the crowded sidewalk outside.

Once clear, Jean tugged at his coat and directed his attention across the street. "She's closing up for the night."

A figure in blue vinyl, slender below the waist, bulging above, was walking from window to window tidying displays and turning off spotlights. The crimson "Pippa's Erotic Gear" faded into darkness just as the lights in the portico below came on, illuminating a polished brass plaque beside the front door. At this distance, Jean couldn't make out the words, but she guessed they read "Lady Niddry's Drawing Room", likely in elegant eighteenth-century script.

"The day shift's ending, the night shift's beginning," Alasdair said.

The lights in the shop went off, leaving the items on show no more than provocative hints veiled by shadow. Below the sounds of the traffic, Jean told herself, that faint whirring was John Knox making like a top even if not actually walking, as an evil presence or otherwise.

Here came Nicola, closing the front door behind her and dodging traffic across the street. She fetched up at the periphery of the group of onlookers, stood on the toes of her high-heeled boots to peer over their heads, then saw Jean and Alasdair loitering a few paces away. She stepped closer. The uncertain blend of light and shadow stripped all color from the elegant perfection of her features, making her look like a marble tomb effigy. "Here, what's happened to the constable?"

Jean caught a whiff of Nicola's perfume, something light

and flowery. Before she could speak, Alasdair weighed in. "He went falling down the stairs."

"Dreadful, but folk won't leave well alone, will they?" Nicola's eye lingered on Jean and her forehead creased with puzzlement. *Where have I seen you before?*

Jean went fishing. "I suppose he was curious about the bodies found in the vault beneath the building."

"Are the police any forwarder with that?" Finding nothing helpful in Jean's face, Nicola focused on Alasdair.

"Somewhat," he replied. "You're in the shop opposite, are you? Have you noticed anything odd?"

"No more than folk gawping, and the police making their inquiries." She turned on one spike heel and strode away toward the university, her blond hair falling across her shoulders like a theater curtain.

"And good night to you, too," Jean murmured.

Alasdair tilted his head first one way—perhaps in appreciation of the snug trousers covering the retreating backside—and then the other, probably defaulting to witness-assessment.

"You noticed," Jean said, "that she knew something had happened to the constable, and she thinks that he or someone should have left well enough alone."

"He was carried away by the paramedics, she'd have seen from her window. Or Bewley was telling her, or . . ." He let his sentence evaporate into the darkness.

Jean got the message. Rational suspicion. "If Nicola MacLaren had mannequins in the window, she'd probably have one dressed like Jason Pagano. Rebecca called him a metrosexual Rasputin."

Alasdair's dry laugh was a good as a guffaw.

"So what does Pagano know, if anything? When did he know it and how and why? And what about Nicola, anyway? Was she fussing at Bewley for lowering the tone of the neighborhood by attracting the police? Or does she know he's been sampling the wares . . ."

". . . oh aye, the man's reeking . . ."

". . . and is regretting having recommended to Vasudev that the fox guard the henhouse?"

"Well then. We should be asking what MacLaren knows as well."

"We?" Jean repeated.

This time it was Alasdair who waved his hand holding the folder in a *never mind* gesture. "Old habits die hard. I'm leaving Knox and Gordon to it. This is us away home. We've got the plans to be going on with."

Side by side, they walked on toward the High Street, Jean filling Alasdair in on her adventures in Greyfriars Kirkyard. "Speaking of proof and its permutations, there's someone else you—we—Knox—could talk to," she concluded. "Robin Davis, a professor of social anthropology at the university. Sara was working with him about the time she disappeared . . ."

The bleat of his phone interrupted her. Jean had never decided whether it was affectation or practicality to set it to the usual British telecom sound rather than a ring tone. With a hold-that-thought gesture at Jean, he plucked the phone from his pocket. "Cameron."

A faint buzz emanated from the tiny speaker. Alasdair's brows quirked, one up, one down. He stepped into the shelter of a doorway, Jean close beside him, and tilted the phone so she could hear. "Aye, that was me."

The female voice said, "You've got a nicer face than that cow Knox. Former policeman, I'm hearing from the duty officer. Protect and Survive. I went ringing them, your chap Ian's gone and given me your number. I'm hoping you don't mind, but I . . . I don't know where else to be going."

"Who . . ." Jean mouthed, then realized who. Amy Herries.

Alasdair's brows tightened, forming that oh-so-familiar crease between them. Whether or not he minded that "nicer face" remark, he applied honey rather than vinegar to Amy's wounds. "Is there something I can be doing for you, Miss Herries?"

"Aye, that there is."

Chapter Ten

Stepping from the chill night into the warmth of the restaurant made Jean's glasses steam up, giving her a moment to focus on the delectable odors of Indian food. She and Alasdair's first—well, it hadn't exactly been a date—had been at an Indian restaurant.

Her vision cleared and she looked around. It wasn't much past six o'clock, early for dinner in this part of the world, and only three tables were occupied. Two students sat in one corner, their backpacks spilling so many books and papers across the table there was little room for samosas and coffee. The couple eating curry in the window were probably Americans, judging by the way they held their utensils.

Amy sat near the back, at a table with only two places. Alasdair hadn't mentioned that his sidekick was coming along to the rendezvous. Making no apologies, he seized another chair and spun it around, seating himself elbow-to-elbow with Jean across from Amy and her glass of beer. "Jean Fairbairn, my wife," he told her, and cut to the chase. "Much better your taking advice from D.I. Knox than from me and mine."

"The cow." Amy meant Knox, not Alasdair's "mine". Jean pulled out her notebook and pen, all the better to play the loyal retainer, and took advantage of the opportunity to jot down a few key words from her Kirkyard visit. Not that she often referred to her notes. The act of writing them helped to embed them in her mind.

"I'm thinking a cop should be having the same slogan as a doctor, first, do no harm. But no, she's up my nose, first telling me it's none of my affair, then telling me it's all my affair and I'd best be airing Sara's dirty linen good and proper."

"Sara had dirty linen to be airing?" asked Alasdair.

A waiter appeared in Jean's peripheral vision. "A menu,

Madam?"

"No thanks, just chai and vegetable pakora. For both of us," she added, when Alasdair's gaze didn't waver from the young woman across the table. Frost gathered on his expression. You didn't rattle Alasdair's cage and walk away unscathed.

Amy's face was no longer as pale as it had been this morning. Her cheeks were polished as much by resentment as by cold, probably, and her dark ringlets—of a shade of charcoal black that couldn't possibly be natural, not with her complexion—bounced with indignation. "Everyone's got dirty linen, eh?"

Alasdair's palms-up gesture acknowledged her point. "And what sort of dirty linen was Sara wearing, eh? What were you not wanting to share with the police? What of that are you thinking contributed to her death?"

Amy leaned back as Alasdair leaned forward, like a twin pendulum. "We were brought up proper, Sara and me. Dundee, a fine place if you're the right sort. And we were, sent away to school in Stirling, then Sara on to uni here in Edinburgh. Me as well, when my time came, but I'm by way of being ten years younger, and Sara was, was gone by then."

"She was twenty when she went missing," Alasdair stated rather than asked.

"Oh aye, that she was. I kept hoping all these years she was away with her boyfriend, still alive in London or even America, but I knew she wasn't. She'd not have abandoned me."

"You were close?" Alasdair asked.

"We weren't of an age to be in school together, so she couldn't help me there. She watched out for me at home, mostly, kept Dad from being as bad a tyrant as he intended. He'd failed with her, he was saying. He'd be damned sure I turned out all right." Amy took a swig from her glass, the quick thrust of her chin indicating obstinacy. A gold chain sparked at her throat, but if anything dangled from it, it was concealed beneath her sweater and blouse.

The gold chain on Sara's body had survived the years much better than her flesh.

"You father said he'd failed with Sara?" prompted Alasdair.

"Oh aye. Last time I saw Sara, alive or dead, she was rowing with Dad about her friends at uni, the wrong sort, he was saying, and her boyfriend the worst of the lot. Immoral, he was saying. Shameful."

"Did you meet this boyfriend?"

"No. Didn't know anything about him. At one time she was seeing an American—and that did him no favors, not with Dad . . ." Sara glanced at Jean. "You're American, are you?"

"Yes, but don't hold anything back on my account."

Amy turned back to Alasdair. "I was away at school, I was ten years younger, Sara didn't confide in me, not any more. Said I wasn't old enough to understand about relationships and all."

"And this man's name?" asked Alasdair.

"They were rowing over someone named Chris is all. I'm not sure 'twas even the same bloke."

Alasdair nodded, no doubt remembering that Knox had said the elusive boyfriend was American, perhaps wondering if Knox had known the name "Chris" at all.

"She wasn't happy 'til she came here to Edinburgh," Amy went on. "Me neither, though it's hard to tell."

Jean wrote everything down. Yeah, it would be hard to tell whether you were happy, if you'd spent your life living up to the expectations of parents who felt your personality was theirs to mold, not yours to develop. "And your mother?"

"Died, years since. It was just Dad, Sara, and me. But she vanished and he died of a heart attack—broken heart, like as not, thinking how he would have done, should have done differently—and now it's just me."

The waiter delivered two cups steaming with cinnamon and cloves, and two small plates piled with savory fritters. Her own flesh suddenly hungry, Jean sipped and munched, balancing the sweet of the drink with the spice of the snack. An elbow in Alasdair's ribs deflected his attention from Amy long enough for him to do likewise.

The young woman's blue eyes were impacted in so much make-up, lined in black with lashes like hedgerows, that they looked inhumanly small. Jean remembered the eye sockets of Sara's skull, inhumanly large, and wondered whether she'd overcompensated the same way. Had her hair, too, been dyed a defiant black? Jean tried dropping a hint. "Was Sara a Goth?"

"She was a bit of everything," answered Amy, "Goth one month, posh the next. Dad said she'd spent a packet on clothes, if she wanted more she could make them herself. So she did. Soon she was making costumes for theater groups and musicians. Me, I can't hardly sew a patch on the knee of my jeans without taking the legs off."

"Was she making historical costumes?" asked Alasdair.

Jean thought first of Pagano's Liz and the cheesy re-enactment in Greyfriars Kirkyard, then of the ghost in the vault. She and Alasdair had never before seen a ghost lingering over its own physical remains, but why not . . .

"Oh aye, she was reading history before she changed to social anthropology."

"Theater groups and musicians," Jean repeated. "I know there were student musicians practicing in the vaults about that time. Were theater groups using the free space then, too?"

"Oh aye. Before the landlords like my Dad moved in with their nightclubs and all," said Amy. "She and her mates were presenting a show at the Fringe Festival, and found themselves a wee theater, but she went missing just at the beginning of August, a week before the opening. Worst possible time."

Alasdair nodded. "In more ways than one, I reckon. The police were distracted by crowd-management during the Festival."

"I'm supposing so, aye. There's no real excuse, is there, leaving her there in the vault, alone." Amy took a pakora from Jean's plate and bit into it, making a satisfying crunch. Jean pushed the plate a little closer to her.

"What play were Sara and her mates presenting?" Alasdair asked.

"'Twasn't properly a play at all, 'twas a satire on the tourists and the ghost tours, though there was a fair bit of history in it as well. Queen Mary and Riccio's murder. Witches burned, Covenanters executed, folk walled up to die of the plague, two-faced Deacon Brodie, Burke and Hare murdering for money."

"Edinburgh through time and space?" asked Jean. "Ghoulies and ghosties and things that go bump in the night, may the Scottish Tourist Board deliver them to us?"

Closing his eyes, Alasdair emitted the sigh of the long-suffering. Jean nudged his knee beneath the table. *Sorry.*

Amy stared. One beat, two—then, with a crack not unlike that of her teeth on the pakora, her face broke into a grin. "Oh aye, that's it exactly. You weren't there, were you now? One of Robin Davis's chums?"

"Who?" Alasdair asked, his knee nudging Jean: *No leading the witness.*

But Jean was bemoaning her owlish appearance, which displayed her academic credentials as clearly as the Greyfriars' guide's name tag.

"Robin Davis, Sara's social anthropology tutor," Amy answered. "He wrote the play. Revue. Whatever it was. She was by way of researching for him. That's what she was telling Dad, at the least, when I'm thinking she was no more than dogsbody or worse."

"Worse?"

"I'm wondering if he's the boyfriend Dad was going on about. Had himself a bit of a harem, I'm hearing, adoring lasses all gathered round."

"A harem?" Jean asked. Michael had said something about Davis being a bit of a goat with the undergraduate lasses. "You mean . . ."

Amy shook her head. "I'm not sure what I'm meaning. Could be Davis was only the mentor, not the boyfriend at all. If I'd known what would be happening, I'd have paid closer attention. I didn't know."

If only I had known. The motto of the human race, right

after, *It seemed like a good idea at the time.*

"Was the play ever performed?" Alasdair asked.

"Once. 'Twas laughed off the stage, and not the way Davis was intending. Music was good, though."

"You saw it for yourself, then?"

"No. I was by way of reading a review in *The Scotsman.*"

"Who was Sara working with? Who were her mates over and beyond the play?"

"I'm telling you, she didn't confide in me."

"Des Bewley?" hinted Jean. "Nicola MacLaren?"

Amy shook her head again, her face registering no recognition.

"Are you minding the names of any musicians?" Alasdair asked.

"Just one, a chap named Skelton. Seemed like the right sort of name, Skelton, skeleton."

"Ah," he said with a nod.

Jean swallowed her own *aha.* Hugh's piper was named Billy Skelton. She wrote the name between two greasy fingerprints and added an exclamation point. "Did she know a man named Jason Pagano?"

"Name sounds familiar," Amy said. "Wait, he's a presenter on the telly, isn't he? Why ever should Sara have known him?"

Alasdair didn't answer that question. His profile, sheened with ice, informed Jean, *There's no evidence Pagano was anywhere near Edinburgh during the nineties. Best be looking for whoever rang him about Sara's body in the vault.*

She almost said, "Yes, dear" aloud, but didn't. Mentioning Pagano was a shot in the dark. A blow in the vault. She was starting to sweat—rooms that she'd call stuffy the Brits called cozy. She should have taken off her coat.

"Chris," said Amy. "That's the only name I'm remembering, and that's because Dad was shouting it so loud."

"You're remembering Robin Davis," said Alasdair.

Amy reached for another pakora. "I don't know what he was to her. More than a tutor, maybe. Maybe not."

Alasdair sent a quick glance toward Jean. She caught it. *Oh yeah. Gotta talk to Davis.* But surely the investigating officer at the time already had.

There was many a slip betwixt an interview and closing the case, Jean reminded herself. No need to remind Alasdair. His lips thinned, the corners tucking themselves in, hiding any vulnerability.

"Did Sara have any special jewelry?" Jean asked Amy.

Amy drained the rest of her beer down her throat and wiped her lips. "She's still wearing the necklace, isn't she? That's why you and the—D.I. Knox are both asking about it."

Jean nodded encouragingly but committed herself to nothing. Alasdair waited.

Reaching into her blouse, Amy drew out a small gold Celtic cross, no more than an inch and a half long but finely incised with interlace even so. "Like this, eh?"

"It's very pretty." Delicately, Jean lifted it, warm from its nest against Amy's living flesh, and turned it toward Alasdair. One of his brows twitched in acknowledgment.

"It's St. Martin's cross from Iona. Mum went there on a sort of pilgrimage when she was first ill, got us each one of these. Seems to me the last time I saw Sara she was wearing something else as well, not gold . . . Ah, I don't know." Amy pulled away, and the cross fell from Jean's fingers.

"Not that I'm at all religious, mind you," Amy said quickly. "Not like Mum and Dad. If there was a heaven they'd be doing John Knox proud. But there's not."

Being certain heaven didn't exist, Jean commented to herself, was no more than the flip side of being certain it did.

"And Sara?" asked Alasdair.

Amy's laugh held no humor. "She was already thinking the church and all was no more than rubbish, even before Davis began telling her there's no such thing as the supernatural, full stop. The world's dark enough, she was saying, without making up stories of evil spirits."

"What about stories of angels?" Jean asked. "The stories we make up . . ."

Alasdair's knee beneath the table stopped her in mid-phrase. He asked Amy, "What is it we can be doing for you, Miss Herries?"

"Find out who killed her. There's someone walking free today who's got away with murder. I don't need religion telling me that's wrong, dead wrong."

"Murder? Who's saying anything about murder?"

"She'd hardly have crawled into that vault and died, would she now?' Amy's eyes flashed in their thickets of lashes. "Don't go asking about drugs and the like. She did her share of mind-altering substances, I reckon, but never so much as to cause her trouble."

A blow to the head, Jean thought, was trouble. A blow leaving a sharp-edged wound.

"Were you telling D.I. Knox any of this? About the theater group? Robin Davis?" Alasdair circled back around to his opening statement. "I'm no detective, not any more. It's Knox who's after finding—finding out what happened to Sara."

Alasdair was still a detective, if of the generic . . . No. Nothing about Alasdair was generic.

Amy shook her head so emphatically her curls bounced and her whole body shuddered. Pulling a couple of pound coins from her pocket, she threw them onto the table. She rose halfway to her feet. "Never you mind, then. I'm seeing how it is. I'm on my own, the way Sara was on her own, left on her own, when she died."

Alasdair murmured, velvet over steel, "Don't be daft."

Amy froze, crouching.

"You've got D.I. Knox's business card, aye? Then you'd best be ringing her, telling her all that you've told us. If you're genuinely wanting to see Sara's death explained, that is."

Slowly Amy stood straight. She looked at Jean. Perhaps tears sparkled on her thick lashes, perhaps the bright lights of the restaurant reflected oddly from her eyes.

Jean tried what she hoped was a stern if reassuring smile. "We'll do what we can to help. But we're civilians. We don't have the resources of the police."

Amy looked at Alasdair, a resource of the police.

"Much better having Knox with you than against you," he said, scooting back his chair.

Reluctantly, she nodded, and, brightening by a match's worth of light, added, "Maybe Knox isn't so bad. I was overhearing two women at her office talking about her, something about that sergeant, Gordon, and a possible sexual harassment complaint. She's overbearing, aye, but there's principles needing defending." Amy looked at Jean.

A what? Feeling her mouth drop open, Jean snapped it shut and nodded agreement. "Yeah, you gotta defend your principles."

"Ta." Amy seized her coat from the next table and fled.

Jean and Alasdair stood up simultaneously. He picked up Amy's pound coins. "Not enough, I reckon."

"Let me." Jean tucked away her notebook, paid for the food and drink, and once again buttoned up her coat.

Outside, the restaurants and bars of the Grassmarket hummed with activity. The open area had once been an animal market. It had been a place of execution. It had been a slum, hunting grounds for Burke and Hare. But time had flowed on, transforming agony into the romance of yesteryear.

Above the lights and the voices, the Castle loomed against the cloudy night sky. One window formed a glowing rectangle. A guard room, Jean supposed. She wondered what it was like, being a night watchman in a place as evocative as Edinburgh Castle. You wouldn't have to be sensitive to ghosts. Like Robin Davis's test subjects, just expecting them would make them appear.

Pagano would get to the Castle, too, she was sure.

"Was Sara," asked Alasdair, "an apt pupil for Davis, then? Or did she come round to his way of thinking for admiration of him—or more?"

"Speaking of talking to Knox . . ."

"I'll ring her soon as we get home."

"Sure, but I mean, what Amy said as she was leaving. Is that what's up with Knox and Gordon? He's been harassing her?"

"None of our business, Jean."

"Well no, but . . ."

Alasdair's hand, firm in the small of her back, guided her toward the West Bow. "Sorry to be signaling you beneath the table, but you're seldom staying with the subject at hand."

"Or what you think is the subject, anyway."

"The subject is Sara Herries' murder."

"You always say yourself we never know what's relevant and what isn't."

"We?" he repeated, the light of a shop revealing his thin smile.

"Right." Huddling into her coat—after the stuffy restaurant, the night seemed even colder—Jean saved her breath for the climb to Castlehill and home.

Chapter Eleven

Jean stood in the dining room window contemplating mortality and the flesh. Ashes to ashes, dust to dust, darkness to darkness, never mind Mr. Edison and his light bulbs, which accentuated the shadows as much as lifted them.

She remembered last summer, evenings lingering like a man with a slow hand, when she could read a book in the Princes Street Gardens until her solitary bedtime. She remembered Texas, where mid-February was almost spring, and you could find forsythia in protected corners putting on yellow blossoms like confetti.

She was no longer in Texas, she was no longer solitary, and, speaking of the flesh, very soon now she was going to have to suggest something for dinner. But first . . . Lifting her phone, she pressed Rebecca Campbell-Reid's number.

"Hullo, Jean," came her fellow ex-pat's voice.

"Hey there. How was the concert?"

"Nice and soothing. Linda fell sound asleep. Michael and I are having our tea in peace and quiet for a change."

"I don't want to interrupt, then."

"No, no, they were saying on the evening news that a constable had been attacked—that's your case, isn't it? Tell all!"

By the way Rebecca's voice went hollow, Jean gathered she'd been put on speaker phone. Not quibbling with "case", she told all, getting in return both munching noises and expressions of interest. Finally Michael's voice said, "Mind you, seems to me someone was putting it about The Body Snatcher that one Fringe show—could've been Davis's—was aiming for shock value, pushing the envelope and all, but that was likely no more than marketing. In any event, nothing came of it."

"Unless it was Sara's disappearance that came of it," suggested Rebecca.

Jean shrugged, even though she knew they couldn't see her. "It's all connected somehow. It's just it's all pretty murky."

If not in the apartment, where every light blazed. And not just for her light-adapted eyes. The child of Fort William and Inverness, Alasdair probably found Edinburgh a bit oppressive—if his comment about the buildings frowning down was any indication. She'd been the catalyst, not the cause, of him leaving the police, but the only reason he was living here was because of her.

She went on, "That's the update. Michael, if you remember anyone from those days named Chris . . ."

"Man or woman?" asked Rebecca.

"A man. Sara's boyfriend."

"There was every name you can imagine," Michael replied, "up to and including ones from Timbuktu. If I'm thinking of any particulars, I'll be in touch, all right?"

"Sounds like I missed some good times," Rebecca said. "How about a stroll down memory lane, dear?"

"Oh aye, dear. Bye, Jean."

"Thanks. Bye." Jean looked around to see Dougie sitting in the kitchen door, paws primly together, head cocked to the side, perhaps less in contemplation of appetite than listening to the music filtering through the wall. A master of the fiddle, among a variety of other instruments, Hugh was now zipping through a set of jigs so cheerful Jean laughed out loud, and danced rather than walked to the kitchen.

Food, drink, dance—some true believers looked askance at them all. But it seemed perverse to assume God had given such pleasure to humanity as no more than temptation, an excuse to exercise denial.

She realized she'd been hearing Alasdair's voice from upstairs, providing stereo sound. " . . . the father was saying he'd failed her . . . lad named Chris is all . . . the father didn't half like her mates at the university . . . oh aye, Amy might could have been telling you all this herself, but she took a scunner to you . . . no, don't be wasting your time doing her for perverting the course of justice . . ."

Flapping her ears like Dumbo didn't do Jean any good. Neither did formulating editorial comments she'd never deliver. She couldn't hear what Knox was saying, even though Alasdair was probably holding the phone a foot from his ear while she responded. Ah well, all in good time.

Jean added to the cacophony by opening a can of food for Dougie. He expressed both gratitude and greed by twining around her ankles, then transferred his affections to the odoriferous plop in his dish.

"Robin Davis, social anthropology," said Alasdair, and after another pause, "The original interviews, eh?"

They could stir-fry some vegetables and serve them over rice noodles, Jean told herself, just to continue the Asian theme of the evening. That would be quick and easy to cook, eat, and clear away.

"Well then," Alasdair said. "If that's the way of it, then . . . No, no problem at all. Good night."

Assertive footsteps came down the staircase. Was this the point where Knox told him to bug off, that the official force could handle it just fine without him? Would he start fuming about being cut out of the case?

Jean turned on the burner beneath a pot of water, threw some vegetables onto the cutting board, and started chopping. The music from next door stopped abruptly, then continued with a series of tentative plinks and smooth swoops as Hugh worked out a passage.

"Right." Alasdair strode through the doorway, picked up an onion, and started peeling it. The pungent scent overwhelmed that of Dougie's meat products but made no impact on the icicles gathered on Alasdair's face like on a granite statue on the Castle Esplanade.

"Right?" Jean asked.

"Gary Delaney was the original investigating officer in the Herries case."

Jean opened her mouth but nothing issued from her vocal cords. She remembered D.I. Delaney only too well. His combative attitude toward Alasdair, colored with the sickly green of jealousy, had made a difficult situation even worse. Not that he and Alasdair hadn't come to terms in the end, but still . . . She tried, "Well, even if Lothian and Borders is a big organization, you'd expect the detectives to talk to each other."

"When Knox went contacting Protect and Survive, she recognized my name from Delaney's report on the Ferniebank case. She's had the cheek to ring him up, asking how she should be going on with me."

Cheek? Or the good sense to check references?

Alasdair seized a bell pepper and ripped out the seeds. "He's telling her I'm good but I'm not knowing when to stop. She's telling me she'd rather have me with her than against her."

"Which is what you told Amy about Knox."

"Knox aye, and Delaney as well, but me, I'm not against anyone." He handed Jean the onion and the pepper and leaned back against the doorway.

You're against criminals. You're against fools. "Oh would God the giftie gie us, to see ourselves as others see us," Jean quoted from Burns. Or misquoted. Her mind was overstuffed with trivia, but she made no claims about its accuracy. "A reputation can cut both ways, you know. We've all got history. We haven't gotten here without having been there first. None of us. If you'll excuse my teaching your grandmother to suck eggs."

Slowly the ice melted from his features, the fissure that was his mouth softened, the lines around his eyes unclenched. In repose, his face wasn't so much nice, in Amy's word, as unthreatening, the regular features nothing remarkable. An undercover face.

It was the mind behind it that would leap out of hiding with blinding brightness and fearsome will.

Jean pushed the cutting board down the work top and handed over the knife, trying not to think of the role a larger one had played in the Ferniebank case. "Here, finish the vegetables while I slice some chicken and get the noodles on. I got hold of Hugh before I called Rebecca and Michael, and he says he'll stop in for a few minutes on his way to tonight's gig."

Alasdair went to work, producing cubes of onion and pepper identical to a millimeter.

"As for Amy," Jean said, "or, more properly, as for Sara, are you thinking what I'm thinking, that Robin Davis is a major player in the case? What if Sara refused his advances, and he got angry? Would she have filed a harassment complaint with the university? What if she told him his play or pageant, whatever they called it, sucked Twinkies, and ditto?"

"No joy, Jean. I was trying something similar on Knox, but she's skimmed the original interviews and is saying there's no suspicion at all attached to Davis. He was at an awards dinner in Stirling the night Sara went missing, and was seen there the next morning as well."

"Stirling's not that long a drive. And it's not as though we know the exact instant Sara went down . . . Well, I expect Delaney double-checked Davis' alibi."

"Aye, no fool Delaney. Still, no harm in your talking to him, eh?"

"Delan—? Oh, Robin Davis."

Alasdair glanced up from beneath his brows. "You were already going on about his new book. An interview with an eye to reviewing it in *Great Scot* would go down a treat."

"Oh yeah, he's definitely in my territory. I'll have Miranda him a call tomorrow morning, set something up. After I drop by *The Scotsman* and check up on that play. Michael says word on the street was that it was pushing the envelope, an over-used idiom if ever there was one." Jean threw chicken and vegetables into the wok and noodles into the boiling water. "You know, Alasdair, what we're not asking is who the man in the vault is. Kazmarek says he was hanged, right?"

"Oh aye." Alasdair gathered cutlery, napkins, and plates. "Between the religious artifacts and the clothing of the ghost, you're thinking he was a Covenanter."

"Oh yeah. The ghost isn't evidence, just an indicator arrow, in a way. But surely the Bible or even the buttons—can you tell time period from buttons?"

"Sara might have done, with her historical costumes and

all."

The music from next door stopped, leaving the bubble of water and the hiss of oil to fill the silence along with the neverending murmur of traffic and voices from outside. The aroma of onions, peppers, and garlic wafted upwards, nourishing in itself. Jean started slicing the bok choy. "There's still no accounting for the old body getting into the vault, never mind Sara's. It's a locked-room mystery."

In the dining room, Alasdair made a noise between a laugh and a snort. "It is that." He wandered over to the window, where Dougie was now licking himself down, and took up a stance indicating deep contemplation—probably less of mortality than of police procedure.

Jean dished up their meals. Beneath Dougie's benevolent gaze, they settled down to eat. Five minutes passed before Jean went on, "Plans of the vaults. You said the ones with the bodies don't exist."

"Not according to any schematics in P&S's files, no. Blocked off early on, I reckon. Out of sight, out of mind."

"As Amy said about Sara."

"Sara's in Lothian and Borders' sights now. And ours." Alasdair used his knife to mound vegetables and noodles onto the back of his fork.

Jean had yet to develop that sort of manual dexterity. You had to be raised British. "The vaults beneath Lady Niddry's have to continue on to the west side of bridge, beneath the Playfair Building. That's how the place was built. Didn't you say you walked to either end of the new—I use the word advisedly—vaults with Gordon?"

"They're likely part of the vault network at the end closed off by a masonry wall. The other end might once have been a cave in the steep ground between the High Street and the Cowgate. Gordon's torch wasn't the brightest . . ."

"I think the dark is just darker down there," Jean murmured.

". . . but the walls look to be natural rock, tied into the corridor with bricks and masonry. There's rubbish lying about, bits of wood and metal and pottery and the like. What archaeologists would be calling a midden, more or less."

"But you didn't see any sign of another entrance."

"No." Alasdair inserted a forkful of food into his mouth, chewed, and swallowed. "What I was seeing was the ghost, the lass, standing there, hands folded and head bent like she was praying. The light of the torch went past her one way, and the other, and here's Gordon not noticing a thing, whilst I went locking my knees to keep on my feet."

"Oh. Well. It's like she was praying for Sara."

"More likely she's praying for the man whose body was with Sara's. Husband? Father?"

"Yeah," Jean said, for lack of anything better, and let the image settle beneath a few more bites before speaking again. "If push comes to shove, you can always get some geophysical equipment in there, looking for cavities and so forth, although I don't guess there's all that good a reason to trace the floor plan."

He swallowed. "As for pushing and shoving, Knox is thinking Bewley coshed the constable, having some reason to be looking at the crime scene. They've not found the weapon, though. Likely it was cleaned and put back with the other tools."

"Bewley would have to have had a stronger motive than mere curiosity. But then, if he's the killer, why open the blocked door . . . Oh. To make points with Vasudev. And now he's worried about some bit of evidence left behind at the scene."

"Sara's gold cross, could be. Or the second pendant or charm, the one Amy's thinking Sara was wearing as well."

"What do you think? Is Bewley the killer?"

"He's telling Knox he never knew Sara. Even if he was knowing her, even if he went smashing her head in, seems to me he'd have many an opportunity to get down into the vaults without committing assault and battery on P.C. Ross. Could've locked the chap in the loo, claiming the door was broken, and had himself a recce whilst the tradesmen were brewing up."

"Good thing you're not a criminal," Jean told him, and swirled the last noodle onto her fork.

Alasdair gave her his best—or worst—we-are-not-amused expression. "Whether or not Bewley's the killer, I'm thinking the killer's still in the area, no matter the years that have passed."

"There's a comforting thought. And here's another one. How involved are you going to get with this? This time the victim's not someone we know, or at least met while alive. And—sorry, Amy—thank goodness for that." She picked up the plates. "Tell me you're not trying to compete with Delaney again. Or with Knox."

"I was never after competing with Delaney, and Knox looks to be competent, never mind the bad blood with Gordon." He took the plates from her hands and headed toward the kitchen, his expression even less amused.

The doorbell rang.

Jean sent an *okaaay* toward Alasdair's retreating back. Let sleeping dogs lie. Saved by the bell. And whatever other clichés she was more at ease using in her thoughts than in her writing.

Yes, the Fairbairn/Cameron household—not a term she was quite used to yet—knew the problems of getting planning permission. It had taken string-pulling by Miranda's unwed but still significant other, Duncan Kerr, to get the go-ahead on combining two apartments into one at Ramsay Garden, which, despite its relative youth, was a historical site. For one thing, since they'd been obliged to leave the exteriors unchanged, they now had two front doors. One was permanently locked and barricaded with a bookcase, making the original entrance hall into a small library—combining their households had meant combining their book collections. Fortunately removing one of the two staircases hadn't been an issue.

Passing the closet that now occupied the footprint of the vanished staircase, Jean opened the functioning front door. Hugh Munro stood on the porch, a fiddle case in one hand, a guitar case in the other, the box holding his concertina tucked beneath one arm. "Hullo, Jean."

"Hi, Hugh. Come on in. Do you have time for drink?"

With his bald head fringed by white hair, a white beard, and a stocky body led by a round belly, Hugh resembled a garden gnome. But very few human beings, let alone lawn sculptures, had blue-gray eyes translucent with a perception both keen and wry. "Afraid not, Jean, thanks just the same. The lads and I are having an early start the night, so as to practice for our debut at Lady Niddry's tomorrow and Saturday. Here's us, moving up the social ladder. No more busking by Waverley Station."

Jean laughed. Even before an admirer left him one of the most exclusive flats in town, Hugh's busking days had passed, not least because, as he often said, it was hard to convince passersby he was in need of their loose change when he manifestly had no trouble obtaining food and drink. "Lady Niddry's? Vasudev Prasad invited Alasdair and me there tomorrow, too."

"Ah, good. You'll be hearing the first pass at our Saturday program. We've not played there since the old Body Snatcher days. Now the place is all tarted up for the carriage trade, I was thinking of starting with 'A Man's a Man for All That'."

"At the very least."

"Hullo, Hugh." Alasdair heaved into sight in time to help Hugh maneuver his instruments through the doorway and stack them in the entrance hall.

Behind them, Jean shut the door. And threw it open again when a woman's scream cut through the night. "What the . . ?"

The courtyard outside the door was dark, if hardly silent— the high walls still held an echo of the scream, fading and dying. Pigeons fluttered overhead. Lights flared above the rooftops.

"It's coming from the Esplanade." Alasdair took the steps to the upper floor two at a time, Jean and Hugh climbing behind him at a slower if no less enthusiastic pace.

All three of them packed into the bedroom window overlooking the Castle. There, illuminated by spotlights, a knot of humanity congealed and parted and congealed again, like a giant amoeba. Jean leaned forward, her breath leaving a ghostly shape on the glass—yep, there was a familiar figure, his black leather garb glistening. "Jason Pagano," she said. And to Hugh, "From the TV reality—if you can call it that—show 'Beyond the Edge'. I've had one encounter with him and his crew already today, in Greyfriars Kirkyard."

"Imagine that," said Hugh at her shoulder. On her other side, Alasdair said nothing. His profile imitated that of the Castle battlements, a serrated edge against the cloudy night sky.

Another scream, if not blood-curdling, at least blood-hiccuping. A light—and presumably a camera—panned to show Liz in her seventeenth-century cap, collar, and apron, now tied to a stake, brush piled to her knees. Pagano stepped between her and the camera, gesticulating, no doubt saying something more dramatic than accurate about the witch-burnings that had once taken place there.

A small fire sprang up on the Esplanade. A dim figure—Ryan?—maneuvered a mirror so that the reflection of the flames was directed into the lens of the camera. At least they weren't actually putting poor Liz in danger, Jean thought. With the camera at the right angle, it would look as though the branches around her feet were on fire. All that was missing was the smoke.

Alasdair asked, "Who's given permission for that fire, eh?"

"Someone whose palm Pagano greased, what do you want to bet? The same someone who's allowing him to profane the exact spot where women died miserable deaths." Jean had a time or two felt a frisson there, the chill on the back of her neck that puckered her senses more than her skin and signaled not so much death as despair.

"I'm thinking I should be rushing out there and playing accompaniment," said Hugh. "But then, that's accepting that there's no such thing as bad publicity."

"There are more songs about battles," Jean told him, "than there are about poor old women condemned as witches. You know, man stuff glorious, woman stuff boring."

Hugh and Alasdair both laughed agreement. For another moment they stood there in a row, hear no evil, see no evil, speak no evil—sensing no evil, Jean thought, meant they'd never appear on "Beyond the Edge".

As one, the trio turned away from the window and walked at a more leisurely pace down the stairs. "You sure you don't want that drink?" Jean asked when they reached the bottom.

"Right tempting," Hugh admitted. "But needs must. What's all this about the old Body Snatcher and our Billy Skelton being implicated in a cold case?"

"The story's getting longer and more complex all the time." Once again Jean took it from the top, this time with Alasdair interjecting a comment here and a correction there. Finally she asked, "Do you remember Sara Herries?"

"I'm remembering the case, aye. The vaults, the streets, the uni were papered over with her photo. But I never met the lass. That I knew," Hugh amended. "But then, chances are Michael Campbell and I passed in the vaults a time or two in those days, and I've no memory of meeting up with him. Who's to know?"

"I bet there was a lot of beer and whisky sloshing about the premises."

"I'm no denying that. But the place was often heaving with people, and the lighting none too good, and, well . . ."

"Who's to know?" repeated Jean.

Hugh glanced at his watch. "Any road, there were loads of lasses hanging about, more than a few of them playing along, not just at The Body Snatcher itself, but bars, cafés, theaters, the lot."

"Theaters," Alasdair said. "We're hearing Sara was working with a theater group, aiming to open a revue of sorts in good time for the Fringe, and that one of their musicians was named Skelton. Might not be your lad Billy, but . . ."

". . . it's worth asking him," concluded Jean.

"That it is. He and I weren't mates then, though I knew of him. And the other way round. I'll have a word with him this evening, all right? If he's remembering anything at all, he'll be phoning."

Alasdair reached into his pocket and handed over the small white square of a business card. "He'll be phoning the officer in charge first, please, just to be keeping up appearances."

"What? Did you pick up a handful of those when you were in her office?" Jean asked.

"Of course."

Hugh held the card to the hall light. "D.I. Wendy Knox. A slip of a lass, is she? One who knows karate or judo, all the better for scoring goals with the criminal elements?"

"She's more like a modern-day Boudicca in her chariot," said Jean.

"Fine strapping lass, then? Ah, those were the days." Without specifying whether he meant the days of the ill-fated Celtic revolt against the Romans, or the considerably less—for people who weren't Sara Herries—ill-fated days of free-wheeling entertainment in the vaults, he stowed the card, gathered up his instruments and set forth into the night. "Later, Jean, Alasdair."

They both called after him, wishing him a good evening, and then stood side by side in the doorway craning toward the rooftops and the Esplanade.

Lights still waved back and forth, and voices rose and fell, but no more screams set the pigeons to flapping. Finally Jean wrapped her arms across her chest, warding off more than one kind of chill, and retreated inside, leaving Alasdair to shut the door on what had been a longer day's journey into night than either had bargained for.

Chapter Twelve

Gavin handed Jean her latte as she swept by, suffused with the cold damp of the morning and the self-righteousness of the early riser. "Thanks," she said, and veered into Miranda's office.

Miranda was just taking off her coat. She greeted Jean with a cheery, "All right then, what were you looking out at *The Scotsman* first thing in the morning?"

Jean gulped, then swished the hot coffee around her mouth, trying to keep it from burning tongue or palate. She could hardly complain to Gavin about it being hot, since hot was coffee's reason for existence, after caffeine, of course. "Robin Davis's show for the Fringe. Sara Herries was working on it when she disappeared."

"I'm recognizing Sara Herries. The rest of it . . . Wait. Davis. *Commerce and Credibility*, that Vasudev was going on about."

Using her cup to shove a crisp new copy of *The Scotsman* off the corner of Miranda's desk—a headline blared, "Body in vault identified as missing student"—Jean set it down and peeled off her coat. "You need to fix me up an interview with him. Not for the book so much, that just makes a great excuse to ask about his relationship with Sara back in 1996."

Miranda sat down and reached for her own cup and saucer—coffee in the morning was an insidious habit she'd picked up as a college student in America twenty years before, her roommate Jean luring her into colonial ways. "So the body's the missing lass after all."

"Oh, yeah." Jean plunked herself down and gave Miranda a guided tour through Thursday's post-work adventures.

Miranda nodded. Her finely plucked brows rose and fell. The coffee disappeared down her throat, hidden behind the high neck of a pink cashmere sweater. "Well now," she finally said. "Constables coshed, ghost-hunters on the prowl, and the tentacles of suspicion reaching even to Hugh's band! Whatever next?"

"Not suspicion," said Jean, who'd put away most of her own coffee and was feeling all the warmer and perkier for it. "Evidence. Next should be Knox and Gordon finding not only who coshed poor Constable Rudolph—dang, Knox used his real name but I can't remember what it is—not only who coshed the constable but also who coshed Sara all these years ago."

"What of Sara's play?"

"Davis's revue, you mean. Short sketches, satire, sort of Benny Hill does the supernatural history of Edinburgh. The title was, 'Ghosts for Fun and Profit', which I like, but according to the review—that would be r-e-v-i-e-w—the satire was much too heavy-handed and mean-spirited, insulting the historical figures who are now supposedly seen as ghosts instead of the people who make a living peddling their stories. Like me, in a way."

"Only in a way," Miranda assured her. "You've had your cynical moments, and Alasdair once made his living from them, but still . . ."

"But still," agreed Jean. "The theater was appropriate to the subject matter. Small and old. It was The Deacon's Neck, named after Deacon Brodie, I bet. Respectable businessman by day, burglar by night, whose neck didn't survive his unmasking. Same time period the South Bridge was being built."

"He was the inspiration for Jekyll and Hyde. And for the pub just down the street from here."

"When it came to inspiration, Stevenson was spoilt for choice. Like Pagano is today, although I don't think he has any literary aspirations." Jean stood up. "The thing is, The Deacon's Neck was in the Cowgate, up against the base of the South Bridge."

"Near to where Sara went missing?"

"Near to where she was found, too. In fact, Alasdair thinks that particular vault may link into a natural cave between the

High Street and the Cowgate."

"Better and better," said Miranda.

"Is the theater still there, do you know?"

"I'm thinking not—likely it was damaged in the 2002 fire—but you'll be finding out, I reckon."

"I reckon so, yes. Time to hit the internet." Jean headed for the door, then spun around. "Oh, and . . ."

"I'll be setting you up an interview with Davis." Miranda turned to her own computer. She did not, after all, have every phone number in Edinburgh in her electronic Rolodex of a smartphone—this one she was going to have to look up.

Jean bustled into her own office and within only a few minutes had determined that no, the theater was no longer there. It was not, in fact, anywhere. It had been struggling financially and the fire had put it out of its misery and its backers out of more than a few pounds.

If management chose to put on shows like 'Ghosts for Fun and Profit', Jean told herself waspishly, no wonder they'd gone under. Speaking of under, as in, the Cowgate running under the South Bridge, what was now occupying the Deacon's Neck space?

A bakery with the less-than-evocative name of Cowgate Bake Shop. All right then. This time, Jean promised herself, she really was going to take a stroll along the Cowgate, in what passed for broad daylight. What she was looking for, she didn't know—well, a sandwich or cookie was always welcome—but she probably wasn't going to find a large X on the wall, and the message, "Sara Herries was here". For one thing, she already knew Sara had been there.

Jean was just turning to her usual day's work when her cell phone emitted a generic jangle. Ha on Mr. Murphy—she'd already dug it out of her bag and placed it on her desk. "Jean Fairbairn."

"Jean, it's Billy Skelton. I've had myself an interesting morning with the polis, thanks to you and yours."

"Oh dear—I didn't mean for Hugh to send you off to the police station so early. Not after a working night."

"Ah, 'twas my own fault ringing Inspector Knox just before last night's show. I was told to be turning up in her office before dawn had fairly cracked. But wee Sara was by way of being a mate of mine, see, and if someone's done her over, then I'm for laying the bastard by the heels. Or by the throat, even better."

Jean visualized Billy's wiry hands dancing delicately on the chanter of his bagpipes, then saw those hands squeezing the windpipe of someone who, as yet, was no more than an amorphous humanoid figure. He or she wouldn't be emitting sweet music under that grasp. "Knox told you they'd identified the body?"

"Oh aye. She's saying the lass was murdered, struck down by a blow to the head. Died on the spot, like as not, but there's no being sure of that."

Jean swiveled her chair toward the window to see light. Watery, frail, tentative light, but light nonetheless. She smelled the dank air of the vault with its hint of smoke. She felt the dark closing in. "Died instantly," she stated. "In a room with an older, dismembered body and a mortsafe."

"Funny, that. I'd never heard tell of mortsafes and all 'til they hired me to play for the show. There was a scene about body snatching, and a mortsafe built of aluminum foil, the sort you'd be wrapping your food in, and Burke and Hare dancing about with it. Not half historical, Sara was telling me, and a load of codswallop, I'm thinking, but they were paying me to play my pipes, and that was rare enough in those days I was saving my breath to inflate my bag."

That scene hadn't been mentioned in the review. A scene involving the ghost of a Covenanter getting it on with the ghost of Mary, Queen of Scots, had been, derisively. "Sara disappeared right before the show was to open?"

"Aye, that she did. Gave me a turn to hear she'd been lying there perhaps no more than a football pitch away, although how she got herself in there's a right good question."

"One we're all asking," Jean told him. "You didn't know there were vaults beneath the Playfair Building?"

"Not a bit of it, no. The tour companies hadn't quite got themselves up and going, then, and the vaults weren't yet mapped out."

"So I guess asking you if the theater had some secret passage running back toward the South Bridge and the vaults is a waste of time."

"It is that, sorry."

Jean tried a different angle "What part did Sara play?"

"She was in the chorus, making costumes, painting scenery, and the like."

"Did you see much of Robin Davis?"

"Oh aye, he was directing, seeing himself as Steven Spielberg, I reckon. Sara fancied herself his assistant, always suggesting improvements. What she was seeing as improvements, at the least. More glitter on the sets, more sequins on the costumes—you'd have thought they were aiming for a Christmas pantomime—and more four-letter words and mock violence all at once. Had to be cutting edge, she was saying, and Davis was agreeing with her."

"Pushing the envelope," said Jean.

"Oh aye."

"Was there something more than a teacher/student or director/minion relationship going on between Davis and Sara, do you think?"

"He had an eye for the lasses, no doubt of that, and they were all hanging on him, but Sara, she had a boyfriend amongst the cast."

Jean sat up so abruptly her chair creaked. The name "Chris" burst from her throat but, hearing Alasdair's voice in her ear—*No leading the witness*—she kept it fenced behind her teeth.

"Well," Billy amended, "there was a lad she was seeing—I surprised them once, snogging behind the cardboard Castle—don't know how official it was. At that age, mind, nothing's particularly official."

Jean had gotten married at that age. She would have done better to have kept it unofficial. "What happened to him?"

"Left Davis a note saying he was away home, to America. We were thinking the two of them went haring away together, never mind her studies. Mind you, I'm not so sure he was ever a registered student. Backpacker, I'm thinking Allsort was, picking up odd jobs here and there. I saw him cleaning The Body Snatcher a time or two. Never knew his real name."

Sara's boyfriend was at The Body Snatcher? Spreading rumors that the show was pushing the envelope?

"Pathetic, Davis was saying, Sara deserved much better than Allsort, but no one was minding Davis any more, not just then, and when the show closed after one performance, we scattered like it had been cursed. I've never seen another soul of them from that day to this. Nor am I wanting to. Not a happy group, for all the show was billed a comedy. The girls quarreling, the boys bumping heads, each and every one of them competing for Davis's attention."

"Why 'Allsort'?" Jean asked.

"His hair was dyed black as soot, like Sara's, but not so recently you couldn't see the roots growing out. Red-orange, they were, like a carrot. His hair looked like the sweet."

"Ah, I see." Jean was not a fan of the striped liquorice candy called Allsorts, but she could visualize the image just fine. And there was something about that image . . .

Billy was still talking. "Me, I was thinking it odd they'd have chucked it all and gone away together—why a bonny lass like Sara'd fancy a scraggy wee guy like Allsort . . . Women, though, they're still a bit of a mystery to me. Then, they were like being an alien species. Not that I've been saying that last to Inspector Knox now, mind, let alone that inspector at the time."

"Gary Delaney?"

"That's the chap, aye. He was right distracted by the Festival crowds—you're knowing how it is, the town was heaving. He was right certain Sara'd gone off with Allsort, and that papering every vertical surface with her photo was all that needed doing."

"Delaney might have checked at the university to see if

Allsort was registered, although sifting through the records for 1996 looking for an American with two-tone hair would be worse than looking for a needle in a haystack. And if he was just a kid backpacking through Europe or whatever, then there'd be no point looking for him at the university at all." Jean jotted a note on a bit of scrap paper, then went ahead and threw the witness several leads. "Was there anyone there named Chris? How about Nicola MacLaren? Des Bewley?"

"Knox was giving me the same names, but no joy. Seems to me there was a Chris visiting one afternoon, but no one working with the show."

Doggedly, Jean wrote down, "visitor named Chris maybe."

"And that's the long and short of it, Jean. Knox was off in a tearing hurry, to the morgue, she was telling that long tall drink of whisky of a sergeant, and the Museum and somewheres else as well, some woman named Pippa, if I was overhearing properly."

Nicola MacLaren. *All right*. And the Museum? Had Knox followed Jean's advice and sent the decayed book there? After all, the vault was someone else's grave, too, and was haunted by a third person—a former person, now an observable memory . . .

Jean realized she was still holding the phone to her ear. "Thanks so much for filling me in. I'll pass all this on to Alasdair, and I'm sure Hugh will want to hear it, too."

"Oh, Hugh's been hearing an earful about it all along. We'll be seeing you at Lady Niddry's the night, he's telling me."

"Yes. Looking forward to it." Jean switched off her phone thinking that she was looking forward to the music, and the food, and to getting dressed up, even, but not so much to the underground venue. But a posh restaurant in a vault wouldn't take her nearly as far from her comfort zone as the vault that was Sara's grave.

Chapter Thirteen

The door opened and Miranda leaned around its edge far enough to pitch a piece of paper onto Jean's desk—which wasn't far, the room was the size of an average American closet. "You've got an appointment with Robin Davis at a coffee bar at two . . . Oh aye, Gavin, just coming."

She poofed out as quickly as she'd poofed in, *Great Scot's* fairy godmother. Smiling, Jean retrieved the paper and noted the address of the coffee bar, two doors down from Blackwell's Bookshop. What, didn't Davis want her in his office? Was he out and about anyway? Did she have a suspicious mind?

Did she have work to do?

She swung back around to her computer and opened up the article on an archaeological excavation in Orkney that she'd started yesterday. But instead of adding words to the space beyond the blinking cursor, she stared. Allsort. Striped hair. Black dye, like Amy's and apparently Sara's as well, covering a head of hair the color of a carrot, on a scraggy wee guy from the U.S. of A . . .

"Holy shit!" Jean grabbed her trusty notebook and skimmed what she'd written about the scene in Greyfriars yesterday afternoon.

Ryan. Jason Pagano's sidekick was a scraggy wee American with carrot-colored hair. Pagano had been mad at him for being late—not long after someone had hit poor Constable Rudolph and pushed him down the stairs. Perhaps Ryan was the one who suspected evidence had been left behind.

Even as Jean opened her browser and typed in "Beyond the Edge", she remembered Des Bewley saying that no one had been in the Playfair Building that day except people who were supposed to have been there. But if Ryan had donned a hard hat and workman's jacket . . . Pagano's website opened up.

Jean cursored her way past smudged photos purportedly of ghosts, staged photos of Pagano and his leather jacket and goatee, and illegible red on black letters slashed with exclamation points like knife wounds. No, she wasn't interested in videos of older programs, thank you, or the scientific basis behind Electro-magnetic Force Field readers or Electronic Voice Phenomena gadgets. It seemed to her as though he was using science subjectively, not objectively, but then, she had taken a bit of a scunner to the man, as Alasdair would say, and wasn't being exactly objective herself.

Aha! There, well down the "About Us" page, in what looked like an eight-point font, was a list of Pagano's crew. Jean's eye worked its way down half a dozen alphabetically arranged names, including that of Liz Estrada, until it reached the last one.

Tristan Ryan.

Ryan was his *last* name. Okay. While he might be the enigmatic boyfriend, he wasn't the enigmatic Chris. Unless, she thought, what Amy had overheard was her father deploring her sister's relationship with a drifter named Tris.

As for people's names, was Pagano really Jason's surname? Using *Great Scot's* internet snooping devices, Jean quickly established that he'd been born Jason Figg in Sheffield, some thirty-eight years ago, and had studied in Liverpool, in Los Angeles—and in Edinburgh.

Oh, good grief. Jean was starting to feel as though the vault beneath the Playfair Building was the dark version of that café in Paris or New Orleans or wherever. If you sat there long enough, everyone you knew would walk by.

Her phone trilled with "My Love is like a Red, Red, Rose". *Good timing.* She started talking as she switched it on. "Alasdair, you won't believe this . . ."

"My capacity for believing is stretching out like an old pair of galluses," he interrupted. "I've just heard from Knox. She's sent the buttons and the book to the Museum, as you were advising, and she's got an answer back."

"Which is?" Jean prompted.

"We've likely identified the man keeping Sara company in the vault."

Jean didn't quibble over that "we've". Close enough. "So who is he? Probably. Possibly."

"The book's a Bible, as you were thinking, and there's a name written inside the flyleaf, along with lines from a verse or two about facing down one's enemies. Ranald Hamilton."

"Ranald Hamilton." A bell clanged in the back of Jean's mind, slowly, like a church bell tolling the age of the dead. "The Covenanting leader?"

"Likely one and the same. Kazmarek's already had a historian in. Seems Hamilton led his congregation away from the state-sanctioned church, into a cave between the King's Wall and the Flodden Wall, where he went preaching against swearing loyalty to the king. Before long the authorities took notice, and he was hanged in the Grassmarket for treason."

"I remember now. Well, I remember reading about him." Leaning back in her chair, Jean scanned her overstuffed bookshelves. The one mentioning Hamilton had a blue spine, she was sure of it.

"Hamilton wasn't only hanged, his body was left hanging 'til it rotted, setting an example."

Jean grimaced. "Or making a martyr, depending on your point of view. How bloody unnecessary, all of it."

"Oh aye." Alasdair's voice grated. "Any road, Kazmarek's not only got the name in the Bible, and the neck broken by a judicial hanging, he's got weathering on the man's bones. Unlike on Sara's bones. She decomposed where she was lying."

"I suppose Hamilton's followers eventually gathered up his bones and—did something with them, if surreptitiously. But damn it, Alasdair, they could hardly have left them in that vault!"

"Kazmarek's turned up bits of confetti or glitter beneath both bodies."

Jean bounced up out of her chair. "Glitter. 'Ghosts for Fun and Profit'."

"Got yourself another by-line, have you now?"

"No, no—that's the name of Davis's revue, the one Sara was working on. I told you I was going to look for the review in *The Scotsman*."

"You did do, aye."

"I found a write-up of the show, and what a hysterical muddle it was, too. I also found the name of the theater—The Deacon's Neck, not far from that vault. It's a bakery now."

"Could be Sara or her friends . . ."

". . . or her enemies—someone murdered her . . ."

". . . were bringing the bones into the vault themselves. Macabre, but there you are."

"Positively gruesome. Part of the same impulse that makes kids vandalize cemeteries, maybe." Jean went back to scanning her shelves. A blue spine. A blue spine. "Anyway, Billy Skelton called a little while ago, after he talked to Knox, and told me about the show, and guess what?"

Alasdair made a sound that was consideration and encouragement combined, and only partially directed at her— she heard Ian's quiet voice in the background. So Alasdair was at his office. No surprise there.

"It was Ryan, Pagano's director or whatever, who was Sara's boyfriend." Jean went on to explain "Allsort's" nickname and the reason for it, and how her train of thought had pulled into a station marked not "Chris" but "Tris", never mind Billy's vague notion that "Chris" actually existed.

"That's leaping to a conclusion," cautioned Alasdair.

"My stock in trade."

"Oh aye, it is that. No harm my passing Ryan's name on to Knox, though."

"Billy said she said something to him about the morgue, the Museum, and 'Pippa'. I figure Knox was planning to interview Nicola MacLaren, since she was going to see Kazmarek and the book conservator anyway."

"Billy was recognizing Nicola's name?"

"No, he wasn't. It's just that she's—there." By now Jean was at the far end of the room, all of three paces away, scanning the shelves about knee level. Aha! There was the book she wanted, with a red spine, not a blue one—go figure. She pulled it away from its closely-packed neighbors. "The thing is, all today's thirty-somethings were here in the nineties, all drawn by the university. Nicola and Bewley knew each other as students. Ryan—assuming he's Allsort—knew Sara. Did Nicola know Sara? Did Nicola and Ryan know each other? Ryan may not have actually been a student, but that doesn't matter. Where does Bewley come in? Innocent bystander, like he claims? We've got one from column A, two from column B, and so on. And what about Davis and his favorites? Was there a love triangle? Who's the hypotenuse?"

Alasdair chuckled. "You're mixing your metaphors. But that's another of your goods on offer."

"Yep." Jean sat back down. "Oh, and Jason Pagano, né Figg, was a student here in Edinburgh for one semester, but a couple of years earlier than Sara."

"Was he, now? Maybe he's your hypotenuse."

"Someone told him the body was Sara's, and that she was murdered, before the word got out."

"He's by way of being the catalyst, then. His bringing his dog-and-pony show to town had Vasudev and Bewley opening up the closed door and, well . . ."

"Here we are. And there Knox is, talking to Nicola. She's on the ball. Or behind the eight-ball, rather."

"Being pressurized into settling the case? Oh aye. She's saying she had a word with Davis as well, to no particular effect."

"I bet she wants to show up Delaney."

"I'll not be putting it past her . . . Aye, Ian, I'm minding the meeting at the university, thank you."

"Gee, you mean you have work to do for P&S?"

"I'm no employee of Lothian and Borders, or *Great Scot*, or Amy Herries, come to that."

"I'll be right up the street from you, then, working for all of the above. I'm talking to Robin Davis at two, at a coffee bar next to Blackwell's. Which is probably no accident. A new book, a bookstore, kind of like, well, love and marriage."

"Right," said Alasdair. "We'll be having us another blether at home, shall we, whilst dressing in our glad rags for tonight's do?"

"Sure thing. See you later." Switching off the phone, Jean picked up her reference book and turned to the index. Hamilton, Ranald. Check. And Hamilton, Grizel?

There's a name you didn't see any more. Wondering if it were a peculiarly, well, grisly Scottish version of Griselda, Jean turned to the page. Ah. Grizel was Ranald's motherless daughter and, at sixteen, his helpmeet. When he was taken by the authorities, Grizel brought food and messages to him in prison. After his execution—quite some time after his execution—she gathered up his bones and buried them. Or did she hide them, along with his Bible, in the cave where he ministered to the aged, the poor, and the sick?

If our ancestors possessed a vindictive streak, Jean thought, *they also possessed great intestinal fortitude.*

Taking her father's place, Grizel had begun to preach. She piled scandal upon scandal by not only espousing illegal ideas, but by being an uppity woman. And in due course she, in turn, fell afoul of the authorities. Rumor even had it that she was turned in by members of her own congregation.

This time, Lord Provost George Mackenzie and his ilk had an even better—or worse—setting-an-example idea. Grizel was thrown from the King's Wall into the valley where she and her father had ministered, like the scapegoat of the Old Testament cast into a valley near Jerusalem. But like killing the goat, killing Grizel Hamilton didn't atone for anyone's sins.

At least this time the other Covenanters were allowed to claim the physical remains and give them a decent burial at Greyfriars.

Jean turned back to the bookshelf, now looking for an archaeological history of Edinburgh. The Covenanters generally met in secluded spots in the countryside, but the Hamiltons, recognizing that the elderly and the sick weren't able to get out into the countryside, stayed in the city. In a cave between the King's Wall and the Flodden Wall. . . .

She opened the book beneath her desk lamp and found a map of the town walls of Edinburgh. *Yes.* The fifteenth-century King's Wall ran south of the High Street, crossing the area now covered by the South Bridge just north of the Cowgate, close to Lady Niddry's and the Playfair Building. The sixteenth-century Flodden Wall ran on the other side of the Cowgate, beyond where the Museum stood now, and angled back toward the Castle past Greyfriars. In the 1680s, the infamous 'Killing Times', the Cowgate had counted as part of the city, but had still been rough in terrain and rough in inhabitants.

The bottom line, Jean told herself, was that poor Grizel had been thrown into the valley of the Cowgate, near the cave where she and her father had held their services. Where she had perhaps hidden her father's bones. What had Alasdair said, about his and Gordon's expedition to the far end of the vault where Ranald Hamilton's bones had been recovered in company with those of a woman three centuries younger?

Something about the walls looking like natural rock, tied into the corridor with bricks and masonry. Something about rubbish lying around, bits of wood and metal and pottery. What archaeologists would call a midden.

Something about the ghost of Grizel Hamilton, head bowed, hands folded.

Closing the book, Jean restored it to its spot on the shelf and reached for her phone and her bag. The conservator might have helped identify the man's body, but she'd just identified the ghost, which—who—was nothing so dramatic as Pagano's Mackenzie Poltergeist, but was a lot more personal. She had to tell Alasdair. She had to run down to the bake shop cum theater . . .

No. She took a deep breath and put her phone and her bag down again. Miranda's pound sterling only went so far, the article on Orkney was due, and Alasdair, too, had a day job. The building and whatever secrets it hid had been there a long time. It could wait another couple of hours.

By which time, Jean told herself with a glance out the window at the darkening sky, rain would again be falling.

Chapter Fourteen

The rain fell. Buses, taxis, and cars swished through streets running with water and pedestrians plodded along, heads down, umbrellas bumping. Jean picked her way from the George IV Bridge down the steep curve of Victoria Street and the West Bow, imagining the pavement echoing hollowly beneath her feet, labyrinths, cellars, vaults, caves, history not only layered vertically but horizontally and diagonally.

She stopped in the mouth of the narrow road that was the Cowgate. It looked like an asphalt canyon lined by buildings, half-obscured by damp and gloom. Now there, she thought, was an area that could use some Las Vega-style neon signs, the gaudier the better.

Passing the oldest building on the street, an almshouse well over a hundred years old when the Hamiltons had known it, she walked under the arch of the George IV Bridge—water droplets like slow tears plunked onto the hood of her coat—and splashed on toward the east and the arch of the South Bridge.

Even on a sunny day the street lay in shadow. Only near the equinoxes would the sun shine straight down the man-made gorge. But the orientation of the Cowgate was an accident of topography, not a religious impulse like the careful siting of Stonehenge, never mind how many religious impulses had been either welcomed or derided here, "Ghosts for Fun and Profit" not even being the most recent.

The dull boxes of modern buildings stood cheek by jowl with Victorian turrets packed closely against Georgian-era pediments, all damp and dour together. As Jean grew closer to the South Bridge she could make out the construction site climbing one side of the arch, new structures replacing those lost to the fire. She wondered if the ghosts and poltergeists and creepy-crawlies had been exorcised, if from the eye of the beholder rather than from any objective location.

There was the Cowgate Bake Shop, just west of the bridge and almost below it. A plate-glass window inserted into a stern stone facade revealed a brightly painted and lit café.

Jean ducked inside, setting a bell on the door to jangling, and stood on the mat dripping and inhaling. Baking flour, fat, and sugar mitigated the damp and dark as much as a cheerful paint scheme. When an apple-cheeked granny in a tidy smock offered her a table in the window, she took it, and ordered tea and a scone, never mind the cheese and chutney sandwich for lunch at her desk.

Jean peered past the glass case displaying breads and pastries into the kitchen, whose ovens, appliances, and work surfaces were as up-to-date as any on a television cooking show. Since she hadn't entirely been joking when she said something to Billy about a secret passage running from the theater back toward the South Bridge vaults, the lack of inglenooks, steel-barred doors, or "Open Sesame" style boulders was disappointing.

The waitress returned with a proper tea, not only a pot trailing the tags of several tea bags, but also milk, sugar, and a plate holding a scone and mounds of butter and jam. Back home, Jean thought, hot tea was a cup of lukewarm water with one bag, dismal as a drowned mouse.

"Thank you," she said, and, as she poured the steaming peat-colored liquid into her cup, "I hear this shop used to be a small theater."

"Oh aye, that it was," the woman replied. "I mind it from my girlhood, not that my mum let us girls stop in. Not wholesome entertainment, she was saying."

"No great loss when it closed, then."

"Well, it had become a student venue, still unwholesome to some folk, I'm thinking, but live and let live."

Jean nodded agreement. "Was the building damaged in the 2002 fire?"

"A wee bit, the owner's telling me, mostly by smoke. 'Twas

in a bad way to begin, mind you. He got himself quite a bargain, buying the old place, but then, he's been buying and renovating buildings all through the area."

"His name wouldn't happen to be Duncan Kerr?" asked Jean.

"No, lass, he's a South Asian gentleman with one of those names my tongue doesn't wrap round too easily."

"Vasudev Prasad?"

"Aye, that's the chap. Friend of yours, is he?"

"We've met. He did a nice job of brightening the place up."

"Ah well then," the woman said with a shy grin, "'tis my daughter and I who leased the shell of the place and fitted it out."

"Well done!" Jean returned. "How old is the original building?"

"Eighteenth century, or near as makes no matter. This entire area was built and re-built when they threw the South Bridge across the Cowgate."

Jean imagined the engineers standing in the High Street and shot-putting the stones across the valley. "So do you have any ghost stories here, like they do in the South Bridge vaults?"

The woman laughed, every crease in her face turning up with merriment. "Ah no, lass. If there were any bogles about the place, the painters and all sent them on their way." The bell above the door jangled as a man entered, and she turned away. "Enjoy your tea."

"Thank you." Jean proceeded to do just that, thinking that one reason for the British fixation on hot tea was that holding the cup warmed your hands. Although she had to set it down long enough to slather butter and jam on her scone.

Chewing the rich mouthful, she looked again into the kitchen, trying to visualize the shell of the building that the woman and her daughter had leased. Had Vasudev had plumbers in here, too? Surely he had. But apparently there had been no blocked doors for them to open.

Not that the Hamiltons had been ministering to the poor

and the sick—exactly as instructed in the Bible that had gone into eternity lying beside Ranald—in a Neanderthal-style grotto. No matter the original appearance of a cave in the steep ground running up to High Street, by the seventeenth century it was no doubt being used as an animal pen, a storeroom, a workshop, or all three. Some paintings of the Nativity showed Jesus born in a cave, not a free-standing stable, a fine point that probably had not escaped either Ranald or Grizel.

A century later the natural enclosure had been connected to the network of vaults beneath the South Bridge, vaults originally intended as storerooms and workshops. She had only Alasdair's paranormal-blinkered opinion that it still looked anything like a cave, albeit floored with rubbish.

Jean turned the other way and looked through the streaming window into the Cowgate. The picnic tables in the forecourt of the pub across the way sat empty beneath dispirited banners advertising beer . . .

The solitary man standing on the curb was Tristan Ryan. She hadn't recognized him at first, with his red-orange hair half concealed by a green and yellow baseball cap. And his pose was no longer that of the in-command, in-charge director. He stood with his hands thrust deep into the pockets of his coat, shoulders slumping, staring at the bake shop as though seeing not its contemporary face but that of the old theater. As though he was seeing himself in an earlier life.

Abandoning her scone, Jean gulped down the last of her tea—it was still so hot it seared her tonsils—and rushed up to the counter. Even though it took her only a moment to thrust several coins at the granny, by the time she shot out into the street, Ryan was gone.

She looked east into the murk, and west into the murk, and, not her thumbs but her shoulder blades pricking, up. Four stories above, a dim figure gazed down at her from the railing of the South Bridge . . . The moment she glimpsed the figure, no more than a humanoid shape swathed in protective garments, it whisked way around the corner of the building. It hadn't been Ryan, not unless he'd learned how to leap tall buildings in a single bound, changing his clothing and headgear as he went.

The falling rain smeared Jean's glasses, and she lowered her face. Was it chickens who drowned because they'd look up into the rain, mouth open? She was no Chicken Little, never mind what Alasdair would call her poultry-in-motion moments, but she was sure the person on the bridge had been looking at her, and not with friendly intent.

Asking questions could be a dangerous business.

The chill that puckered her shoulders had nothing to do with the weather. She tried a deep breath, only to suspect that the fumes of every internal-combustion engine in the city had settled into the valley. Crossing her arms protectively, she abandoned the Cowgate and climbed a few paces up the perpendicular furrow of Blair Street.

No, there was no alley or wynd running behind the bake shop and its neighbors, only a courtyard holding plastic crates and garbage bins. A door freshly painted bright green opened from the shop itself. In the wall at the back, virtually beneath the bridge, stones outlined the ghost of an archway, perhaps an old stable door. But those dingy stone blocks with their coating of lichen hadn't been moved for far, far longer than fifteen years.

On up Blair she went, back toward the High Street, her footsteps slapping on the sidewalk. Behind these buildings lay some of the most notorious vaults, haunted not by George Mackenzie but by another evil spirit, Mr. Boots, known by his heavy steps. Just recently a tourist had been hit so firmly on the head the tour company filed an accident report. Probably the man had walked into a low lintel in the darkness. Surely the company hadn't gone so far as to wield a blunt instrument themselves.

Though you never know, Jean told herself as she cut through Hunter Square, behind the Tron Kirk, if not so much about ghosts, then about motives. And mysterious figures on bridges.

Speaking of figures, of the hour-glass variety possessed by

managers of erotic gear shops, with Ryan attracting her away from her scone she still had half an hour's leeway before meeting Davis. She might as well make her venture out into such disheartening weather worthwhile.

She darted across the South Bridge, took a right past the shops and their glaring lights, hurried alongside the thick stream of traffic, and pulled open the tidy brass-and-glass doors of Lady Niddry's.

The entrance hall was paved with black and white tile. Even though it wasn't lit, a chandelier with curving brass arms drew her eye up the sweep of the staircase. Right now only the faintest odor of cooking competed with the scent of cleaning compounds—no mildew at all, well done, minions of Vasudev. Jean cast a glance at the closed double doors to the right, and an ear toward the chime of crystal and silver emanating from behind them. Her taste buds did a few jumping jacks of anticipation.

In the meantime, there were other ways of honoring the flesh. She headed up the staircase toward a hot pink sign reading "Pippa's Erotic Gear", and on the landing smacked against an icy force field.

Cold, heavy, the back of her neck pleating—yes, there was a ghost here all right, if not a visible one. If not a particularly sorrowful one, either. Jean sensed a calmness that made still water look like shallow rapids.

Grizel? Sara? Or someone else? Whoever it had been, there was nothing she could do now for its disoriented soul. Pushing past, she burst into Pippa's so abruptly a shop assistant and two customers looked around.

"Good afternoon," Jean said with what she hoped wasn't a wild-eyed smile, and turned to the nearest display case. Jewelry. Silver spider webs glinting with rhinestones. Chokers with red beads implying vampire bites oozing blood. Rings and studs for body piercings. Decorative handcuffs, a term that was apparently not an oxymoron.

Taking a deep breath of the sweet, musky atmosphere, she raised her gaze. And realized she didn't have nearly the imagination she'd always thought she had, the one other people had often accused her of having.

The shop looked like a faculty club twinned with Victoria's Secret, wood paneling and polished glass presenting garments in styles and fabrics that had no pretension to practicality, only to a cheerful carnality. Candles, oils, massagers, DVDs and books, a rack of foil packets all packaged tastefully and yet provocatively. She was pondering the uses of a selection of straps and buckles when Nicola MacLaren arrived at her side.

"Good afternoon, madam. May I help you find . . . It's you, is it?" Today Nicola was playing not the vixen but the businesswoman. Her hair was twisted into a smooth French roll on the back of her head, and she wore a lightweight tweed jacket over a pencil skirt and low-heeled shoes. All she needed was a pair of glasses to complete the transformation. But she didn't need glasses to focus on Jean's face. "You were just outwith the Playfair Building yesterday evening. And in the morning as well, chatting with P.C. Ross. You don't look like being a reporter. Or the police."

Part of Jean's mind noted that once again her appearance revealed her profession—or former profession, at least. Another part noted that Nicola knew Constable Rudolph's name. "I'm a journalist. Jean Fairbairn, from *Great Scot*. I've been trying to find out more about Sara Herries, how she ended up in the vault. Did you know her?"

Nicola's lightly made-up eyes narrowed. "I had the police this morning, asking the same questions. I've you to thank for that, have I?"

"They always ask questions of everyone in the area."

"There are plenty folk in the area."

"Yes, like Des Bewley across the street, who helped to open the blocked doorway in his basement. Vasudev Prasad says you know him." Jean dropped the name of Nicola's boss like a cat dropping a dead bird at its owner's feet.

Nicola blinked. "Ah, yes. Des and I were at university together."

"With Sara Herries?"

"Yes."

"Do you know what happened to her?"

Nicola's gray eyes fixed Jean, clear and steady. This time it was her rosy lips that narrowed, so much so that her words barely escaped the fissure. "Something dreadful, there's no doubt of that, is there? Now if you'll excuse . . ."

"Do you know Jason Pagano from 'Beyond the Edge'? How about his associate, Tristan Ryan?"

"Vasudev has given them permission to film at Lady Niddry's the evening."

That didn't answer Jean's question, but was an interesting factoid in its own right. Perhaps Nicola offered it up as a distraction.

Nicola spun toward the two exiting customers, each carrying a pink shopping bag tied with ribbon. "Thank you for visiting."

The two girls—and they were girls, to Jean's eye—giggled and grinned and walked out the door. Nicola made a feint after them, but Jean had another question. "Did you check out Bewley's bar yesterday afternoon, maybe have a chat with the constable on duty?" Which wasn't quite as direct a question as "Why did you know the constable's name?" but might get a reaction even so.

Nicola, her shoulder and profile now facing Jean, said to the case of jewelry, "You've got a lot of questions."

"Asking questions is my job."

"How amusing for you," Nicola retorted. "I stopped in to see how Des was getting on. Not the strongest chap, Des. All this has shaken him. It's shaken all of us, eh?"

Well yes, Jean could buy that. Although why should Nicola feel protective of Bewley? Some past history? Before she could frame that as a question, Nicola strode off toward the back of the shop. "Please excuse me, Ms. Fairbairn, I have a variety of duties to see to, for Vasudev and others as well."

Clever, to throw Vasudev's name back at her. And it wasn't as though Jean didn't have somewhere else to go, too. Or that Knox hadn't asked many of the same questions.

"Thank you. I appreciate your taking the time," Jean called, but Nicola had already disappeared behind a door marked "Staff Only".

The shop assistant was folding filmy bits of garments, her back turned, although Jean suspected her ears had rotated around like a cat's. "Thank you," Jean threw to the scented air, and fled past the chilly spot on the landing, down the stairs, and out into the cold rain.

Chapter Fifteen

Buses, cars, taxis, even a couple of drenched motorcyclists sat idling in the street. Thinking of the silence of the coast of Skye, the sound of seabirds and the scent of fresh air, she dodged between the vehicles and gained the opposite sidewalk. There, she cast a suspicious glance into the construction site that was the Resurrectionist, but saw no Des Bewley and no constables, although Knox probably now had two of them stationed in the cellar.

Jean whisked past the balustrade protecting the gap over the Cowgate without looking down, but did pause outside the door of the appointed coffee bar to gaze toward the Old College. By this time Alasdair was there at the university, occupied in gainful employment. She didn't need to call him and report her progress snooping, gainful or otherwise. You'd think she was a newlywed or something.

The waiting vehicles jerked into movement, sending up bow waves of water, and she ducked into the shop with its scent of coffee, more delectable than all the perfumes of Arabia, or at least of Pippa's.

Jean looked around the crowded room—gainful employment seemed to be a rather loose concept, except for the baristas busily steaming and pouring—how was she going to recognize Davis . . .

Oh. No problem. That gray-haired, square-jawed guy in the corner had to be him. Who else would have a copy of *Commerce and Credibility* fanned open to stand on the table in front of his cup? Jean threaded her way toward him, shedding her coat as she went. Setting down his tablet computer, he bobbed up and down again, polite if perfunctory. "Miss Fairbairn, I presume. Or are you one of those women who prefers Ms?"

"Jean will do nicely," she replied, without rising to the bait.

"Then I'm Robin. Rather an infantile name, but there you are."

She threw her coat over an empty chair and sat down. And realized she'd seen him before. He was the man taking photos of Jason Pagano at Greyfriars yesterday, the one Ryan had asked to cease and desist.

"Please allow me to buy you a coffee," Davis went on.

"Thank you, but I just had tea. Inhaling the odor is almost as good." Jean felt like the little match girl laying her tattered paper notebook next to Davis's spiffy tablet, now glowing with a screen saver of—wait for it—the cover of *Commerce and Credibility*. Such as it was. The illustration, an eighteenth-century etching of a man quailing before a ghost that was clearly a sheet manipulated by wires, was no larger than postage stamp, and was hardly visible in the blocks of type proclaiming title, author, author's titles, and a quote or two from other be-titled names, all on a mustard-colored background. But she wasn't here to offer opinions on cover design.

Davis spun the book around, opened it to the title page, and signed it with a flourish and a smile, a rectangle of dazzling if crowded white teeth. "Here you are. I'll be interested to hear your opinion, since you write about this sort of imbecility yourself. My studies have shown that people see what they expect to see . . ."

Or what they're guided to see, Jean told herself, giving Davis the twice-over. Even though his jaw only seemed square because it was thrust up and out belligerently, he wasn't an unattractive man. His gray hair was expertly cut and styled, his tweed jacket and regimental tie implied intelligentsia rather than fustiness, even the stomach slightly distending his waistcoat and the chain of a pocket watch gave him a benign appearance, like Winnie-the-Pooh contemplating deep thoughts.

Winnie-the-Pooh, Jean thought. Robin Davis. Christopher Robin. Chris.

Oh come on, now. Everyone can't be the damned elusive Chris.

Davis was still talking, his dark eyes so meltingly sincere

he'd never noticed she'd tuned out. ". . . make our own reality. Don't you agree?"

If ghosts are no more than creations of our own minds, why do Alasdair and I see, sense, feel exactly the same thing? "I agree that experiences with the paranormal are for the most part subjective, and people do often see what they expect to see. But in my . . ." Jean changed "experience" to "opinion" in midsentence. ". . . there's a perceptual tidal zone between experience and objective reality, not a definitive line."

Davis gestured gracefully. "That's the trouble with opinion, isn't it? It's subjective. Especially when it comes to the supernatural. Ghosts in the dungeon or the holy ghost, there's no difference. And yes, I'm well aware that in past times, people were foully murdered for saying just that. Thank goodness for a secular society."

Jean skipped pontificating on the difference between paranormal and supernatural and the history of thought in each area. "Do you confine yourself to ghosts in the dungeon in your book? Or are you tackling religious belief as well?"

"The latter is outside the scope of my studies, mass rather than personal delusion."

"No pun intended?" Jean wrote in her book.

"Pun? Oh, 'mass', I see." His rectangular smile gleamed again.

"Did I see you at Greyfriars Kirkyard yesterday afternoon, taking photos of Jason Pagano and his film crew?"

"Why yes, you did. Well observed, Jean. Cynical lad, Pagano, selling out the truth for a fast—buck. You're American, aren't you?"

"Yes. Do you know Pagano personally?"

Davis shuddered. "I have better things to do with my time than cultivate the acquaintance of someone like him. My book will expose him and his sort for the charlatans they are, as a public service."

A public service, Jean told herself, that will hopefully make you lots of bucks, pounds, euros, and all. "You don't see any usefulness in Pagano and his sort, ah, exposing their viewers to history?"

"Perhaps, if only to demonstrate the foolishness of believers who not only murder but die, all in the name of psychotic belief."

"Psychosis is a strong word. Does that mean you believe . . ." Jean emphasized the word, ever so slightly, ". . . that all guides to the paranormal are cynical exploiters rather than believers themselves?"

"Not at all. Some of these folk, that woman running Mystic Scotland, for example, are simply deluding themselves."

Knowing "that woman" as she did, Jean did not disagree. To hide her bemusement, she glanced toward the window of the café—and realized someone was staring back at her through the wet glass. But the moment she registered the blurry shape, it was gone, as quickly as though plucked away on a bungee cord.

Okaaay. Was that the same someone who'd been watching her from the bridge? Someone who was judging her by the company she kept—and she didn't mean Davis, but Alasdair, and Knox and Gordon. Busybodies are us, she told herself.

She rotated back to Davis. Time to bring the interview around to Sara. "Was 'Ghosts for Fun and Profit' a good use of your time, fifteen years ago?"

"You've heard of that, have you now? What is it they say about good intentions?"

"That they pave the path to hell?"

He hadn't actually wanted an answer—he was still talking. "Throughout history, humor has been a way of educating the common people. I thought an exercise for my students, an amateur production, might open a few minds. But their ideas, enthusiastic as they were, simply weren't sufficiently well thought-out. Not at all like *Commerce and Credibility* with its professional reviews, references, and qualifications."

"It was their fault," Jean wrote in her notebook. "Did you know that Sara Herries's body has been found? She was one of your students, I—well, I don't believe. I know."

Davis acknowledged her play on words with a smile that

was more of a triangle, one that settled into a grim line. "I've not only read the newspaper today, I've had a conversation with Detective Inspector Knox. Now there's a woman who's giving feminism a bad reputation."

No way would a diversion into gender politics end well. Jean wrote "l"—listen.

"Dreadful, poor little Sara lying there all these years. And here's me, thinking she'd run away with that American lad, Allsort, we called him. I didn't even know his real name, so could hardly make inquiries. I was quite sure it was no more than a dalliance on her part, a pathetic choice for a girl of her talents, but when she never reappeared I convinced myself she was happy in that brave new world across the Atlantic. Alas, poor Sara. She should have died hereafter."

Jean mentally checked off his references to *Hamlet* and *Macbeth*. "Did she have another boyfriend? A lad named Chris, perhaps?"

"There's a common name for you." With a heavy sigh and a crumple of his lips, Davis patted the book. "For shame, Jean. I trusted you when you said you were interested in this, this ill-favored thing, madam, but which is mine own."

A spark in his eye dared her to recognize the source of that quote. She did. This one was from *As You Like It*, a character speaking of his wife as a thing. Jean had always been attracted to another phrase in the same speech: *As marriage binds and blood breaks.* But she while she was normally up for a quotation smackdown, this wasn't the time or the context. "Oh, I'm interested in your book, all right. It's just that you have more to offer our readers than your theories on the paranormal."

"That I do, yes." His winsome expression faded, overtaken by self-satisfaction. Leaning back in his chair, he pulled out his pocket watch. Something tumbled after it and swung back and forth on the chain—a small silver skull. "I beg your pardon, I'm expecting my public relations consultant any moment. She's arranging a book launch at Blackwell's . . . Ah." His gaze followed Jean's to his stomach.

"Interesting charm you have there." She concealed her

121

smile at the affectation of the watch. She might still smell of academia, but he was deliberately dousing himself with it.

"Ah. Yes." He returned his watch to its pocket and fondled the skull between thumb and forefinger. "It's a bit of symbolism for myself and my students. I give these out as gifts to the cream of the crop, fittingly engraved with their initials and the date. A *memento mori*, right?"

"Remember you will die," translated Jean.

"A reminder to us among the living to enjoy ourselves now. We have only the one chance to appreciate the flesh, and when it's gone, it's gone. Nothing lingers, no spooks, no spirits."

"The flesh isn't necessarily gone, just the consciousness within it."

"My point exactly. Enjoy sensation and consciousness whilst you've got it. But squeamishness about the body is a characteristic of the religious, isn't it? Especially the more virulent of the Protestant Christian denominations. The Catholics seem to accept the body only after death, when they can play with the *disjecta membra*. As for the Muslims and Jews and all, well, let's not go there."

Did Davis know Sara had found Hamilton's body? Assuming that's what had happened—Jean wasn't at all sure the scenario had played out that way. She was, however, starting to suspect that Davis saw himself as the male version of yet another of Edinburgh's literary characters, Miss Jean Brodie, who also had her favorite students. Davis's chocolate brown eyes with their carefully cultivated blend of sexuality and intellect no doubt appealed to young women. They would have appealed to Jean, if she'd been young, and naive, and not committed to the clear ice-blue gaze of someone who was no longer young and naive either.

Her own hand, displaying engagement and wedding rings, closed her notebook and tucked it away. "Did you give Sara one of those skulls?"

"Yes, I did. I wonder what happened to it? Perhaps it's in a box at the family home."

Or perhaps that's what Amy had seen her sister wearing along with their mother's gold cross, and it still lay in the vault. A tarnished nubbin of silver would look a lot like a pebble— unless you knew what you were looking for.

Jean blinked. She wasn't underground, she was in a busy coffee bar. Davis was tucking his tablet into its leather case. She got the message. "Thank you very much, Robin. I'll be on my way, leave you to your public relations planning. Who is your publicist, by the way? My partner, Miranda Capaldi, is always on the look-out for someone good."

"I'm happy to recommend her." Reaching into an interior pocket, Davis's long, spatulate fingers produced not a rabbit but a business card. He extended it across the table. "If there's anything she or I can be telling you about *Commerce and Credibility* . . ."

"Thank you. I'm sure we can mention it in our books column, since you're a local author and all." She took the card, glanced at it, and aimed it toward the exterior pocket of her bag.

Whoa. She jerked it back again. The card read, "Prasad Public Relations, N. C. MacLaren, consultant", above a phone number and email address. "Nicola MacLaren is your publicist? She is quite versatile, isn't she? How long have you known her?"

"Many years. She took a few courses from me in her university days, all the better to further her business degree. Public relations, social anthropology, they're not mutually exclusive. She's a canny one about the Edinburgh market. In fact, she's introducing me to a few important folk at Lady Niddry's Drawing Room tonight. In the meantime, though . . ." Again with the watch. ". . . we're meeting the management of Blackwell's in just a few minutes. It's been a pleasure, Jean."

"Nice to meet you, Robin," she returned, and, manipulating bag, book, and coat, stepped back out onto the sidewalk and turned toward the High Street and the office.

Part of her mind was registering the rain. The dark. An early evening. Traffic. Pedestrians. Umbrellas. The Cowgate, a shadowed chasm far below. The rest of her mind spun like a Catherine wheel, sparks shooting out into the gray day.

N. C. MacLaren. What did that "C" stand for? Catherine? Cecilia? Or perhaps . . .

Jean felt a stone wall of preconception collapsing, the clouds of possibility rising to fill her vision. She plunged into the loosely formed line of people waiting for a bus in front of the Playfair Building without seeing them as more than shapes in the murk—juggling Davis's book, she reached for her bag and her phone—she really, really needed to touch brains with her other half . . .

An engine roared behind her. The crowd surged toward the street, carrying her sideways. Water sprayed over her feet and legs. Something hard and fast yanked at her right shin, jerking it out from under her. She started to fall, not onto the sidewalk but over the curb into the street.

The book flying out of her hands. Voices shrilling. An ear-splitting squeal of brakes and the smothering odor of diesel. The metal mountain of the bus striking her right shoulder. Hands seizing her left arm and shoulder, yanking her back from the brink to crash against an upholstered surface.

She found herself standing in a clearing, only the hands on her shoulder and arm holding her upright—her legs had turned to Jell-O, her mind echoed in an empty head . . .

She focused. Of the open mouths and staring eyes encircling her, she could make out only two complete faces. Tristan Ryan, his red hair, green and yellow baseball cap, and stark white face contrasting with the black leather garb of the man who was clasping her against his own chest.

Jason Pagano.

Chapter Sixteen

Jean's legs and feet were goose-pimply with cold and wet. Her right shin ached. Her left arm ached. Her neck and shoulders ached. Surely she'd have noticed someone beating her up . . .

Oh. Yeah.

Oh my God.

Pagano half-carried, half-dragged her through the doorway of the Playfair Building, brushing past Des Bewley. Bewley carted a chair from the construction zone into the entrance hall. Pagano plunked Jean down on it. He groped in her mini-backpack—look at that, it was still draped over her shoulder. He found her phone, inspected the screen, asked, "Alasdair. He's the hubby, eh?" and at her weak affirmative nod alerted her husband that he'd come within a hair's breadth of widowhood.

Bewley stared at Ryan. Ryan stared back. At last Bewley muttered beneath his breath, "Allsort?"

A constable galloped up the stairs from the cellar, phoned emergency services, and administered crowd control.

Someone handed her a hot mug. Someone else set the now torn and muddy copy of *Commerce and Credibility* on the floor beside her. Pagano poked at it with the toe of his boot. "Fan of Davis's, are you? You were at Greyfriars yesterday, taking the mickey."

Her thoughts flapped like bats in the echoing cavern of her head. She stared down into the mug and saw that it was filled with milky, sugary, industrial-strength tea. She really didn't want it—her stomach felt like a small boat on a choppy sea—but at least it was warming her hands.

Oh. Yeah. Pagano.

She knew she hadn't meant to give him a hard time at Greyfriars. But by the time she'd formulated the words, the opportunity to say them had passed. An ambulance pulled up outside. A bus pulled away. More police people arrived. Third time's the charm, Jean thought. Fourth time. However many times they'd rushed to this building, called out to serve both the quick and the dead.

". . . places to go, things to do, people to see," Pagano told the constable. No, it was another one, they all looked alike in their key-lime-pie jackets and caps with checkered bands. The officer replied, "Not 'til we've taken your report, sir."

A paramedic told Jean what she already knew, that she would be bruised and sore but was otherwise all right. Physically. "We'll has us a visit to Casualty," she assured her.

"No," Jean replied. "I don't need to go to the Emergency Room. Thank you anyway. I'm all right."

The woman looked dubious, but packed up her kit and departed without arguing.

Jean sipped at the tea, willing the warmth and the sugar to do its job, and looked across the room at Ryan. Was her face bleached as white as his? "This time I wasn't clumsy," she told him. "This time someone tried to kill me."

"Say what?"

"Greyfriars. Yesterday afternoon. You kept me from falling onto the mortsafe."

"Oh." He shrank back into the shadow cast by his boss.

Alasdair catapulted through the doorway, swept aside the constable, and fell to one knee at Jean's feet. Now there, she thought, was an unusual pose.

His eyes blazed, his cheekbones flamed, his breath came in ragged gusts. He'd probably run the three or four blocks from the university. From hair to coat to shoes, he was drenched. Drookit, he'd have said. She felt the chill damp radiating from him as he took her hands in his icy ones. "Jean."

"I'm okay."

"You're sure of that?"

"Someone tripped me. I almost went under a bus. He pulled me back." She indicated the hulking figure inspecting the door into the cellar, raindrops still glinting on his black leather shoulders, and his colorful, slightly built companion. "The guy with Pagano, it's Ryan," she whispered. "Allsort, I think."

"Who tripped you?" Alasdair also spoke in an undertone.

"I have no idea. It was dark, it was raining, it was crowded, and I was distracted by something. Nicola's middle initial. Maybe she tripped me up—I went into her shop earlier—but if Davis could have rushed back from Stirling the night Sara died he could have rushed down the sidewalk from the coffee shop. Or Pagano did it himself, or had Ryan do it, you know, making himself look good for his show. The, ah, black knight saving damsels in distress."

Alasdair's eyes crossed slightly. "Oh aye," he said soothingly. "We'll get it sorted." His gaze turned to Bewley at his usual post, hard hat, truculent expression, wet trousers and shoes. A raincoat lay over a box just inside the door of the pub. "Where was he?"

"He was at the door when Pagano hauled me inside."

"Right." With a squeeze, Alasdair released her hands and stood up. The red was draining rapidly from his face, leaving it ashen. In two paces, he was across the room and in Bewley's face, never mind that the man was two or three inches taller. "Who was after killing my wife, eh?"

Bewley's expression went from truculent to combative, and his red-rimmed eyes glared. "How the hell am I knowing that? I'd just stepped outside, having a look at the weather. Filthy day, everyone's head-down. Next thing, the bus is braking, the women are screeching, and that oik's dragging her in here like a sack of cement."

Pagano and Ryan turned to watch. So did the constable at the door. Jean took a deeper drink of her tea and for a moment wished she had some popcorn.

Alasdair took a step forward, backing Bewley against the wall. His voice softened into a menacing growl. "I'll thank you to be minding she's no sack of cement."

Bewley's Adam's apple jumped. He held up his hands—*I surrender*. "I didn't mean anything. I'm full up, just, with all this happening on my doorstep."

"That makes two of us. Three." Alasdair's right hand gestured toward Jean. His left beckoned toward the cellar door. "You. Ryan."

Obeying the directive in Alasdair's glacier-blue eyes, Ryan stepped forward a few reluctant paces. "Yeah?"

"I'm hearing you had a wee blether with D.I. Knox earlier the day."

"Yeah."

Looming up behind him, Pagano deployed his resonant voice. "Good timing, that. I've got a production schedule to meet, I need my entire crew . . ."

"Bad luck," Alasdair retorted between his teeth, and turned back to Ryan. "I'm hearing you were biding here in Edinburgh in the nineties. You were answering to a nickname. Allsort. I'm hearing you were Sara Herries' mate. Maybe more. You were seen having a wee bit snog with her."

Jean noted that Pagano's face, while still resentful, registered no surprise at this stroll down memory lane.

"Yeah, I was here. I was doing odd jobs, like working as a janitor in The Body Snatcher, where Lady Niddry's Drawing Room is now. Sara got me a gig helping that pompous idiot Robin Davis with his show. But Sara was only—there were lots of girls, and lots of drink—and more," Ryan said with a sideways glance at the constable, who so far was keeping an admirably neutral expression even as he rocked back and forth on the balls of his feet, ready for anything.

"Sara was nothing special to you, was she?" Alasdair took another step forward. "Why'd you leg it when she went missing, then?"

"I was scared. I didn't know anything about how the police work in this country. I thought maybe I'd be framed for something, being the outsider." He shrank back one pace, then two. Behind him Pagano folded his arms and in an elaborate dance step, moved out of the way.

"Who else were you mates with?" Alasdair demanded.

Ryan shrugged, and his shoulders remained up around his ears. "Nobody."

"A woman named Nicola MacLaren? Des Bewley here?"

"Never heard of either of them. No offense," Ryan said to Bewley.

Bewley scowled, but before he could speak, Jean did. "Mr. Bewley recognized Mr. Ryan as Allsort just a few minutes ago."

"Oh aye," said Bewley. "Hair both black and red. Cleaned the old Body Snatcher and filled in behind the bar. Used to go repeating the odd bit of gossip, didn't you now, Allsort?"

"There were lots of people in and out of there," Ryan asserted, his voice rising. "Poor lighting. Loud music. Drink and drugs. Why would I recognize anyone in particular?"

"Sara Herries, now," Bewley went on. "Never saw the woman 'til they carried her up from the cellar in a body bag."

Had you heard of her, though, Jean wondered.

Pagano raised a slab of a hand—a good thing, his having huge hands—and laid it on Ryan's shoulder. "Whoever you are, Alasdair, we've got work to do. Either ask us what happened out there in the street or let us go. In any event, stop harassing my assistant."

"I do beg your pardon. I'm Detective Chief Inspector Alasdair Cameron, Northern Constabulary, retired. What happened in the street, then?"

Ryan spoke up. "We were considering camera angles, we need footage of Lady Niddry's . . ."

". . . and your lady here tripped and like to have fallen in front of the bus," interrupted Pagano. "Fortunately I was standing just there, and was able to pull her back."

"Thank you," Jean said.

Pagano's goatee encircled a quick flash of white teeth. "'Tweren't nuthin', ma'am, as you Yanks would say."

"Thank you," said Alasdair. "And for phoning me as well. What tripped her?"

"So far as I could tell she fell over her own feet."

Ryan added helpfully, "She almost fell over one of the mortsafes at Greyfriars yesterday."

I had to remind him of that . . . Aha, here was her chance to throw out bait. "Yes, I did. I missed my step when you told your boss here that it was Sara's body in the vault, and that she'd been murdered."

Ryan's white face went an ugly ashy green. "It was in the newspaper. Boy, did that give me a turn. Poor Sara, after all these years."

So it *was* him who'd been talking to Pagano in the dusky kirkyard, not someone on the phone at all. Which wasn't a piece of information she'd have wanted to die for.

Alasdair's narrowed eyes registered how that shot had gone home. "The notice was in this morning's paper, not yesterday's. A bit quick off the mark with the details, weren't you now?"

"I—I—well, I've been busy, the newspapers kind of run together, you know—I saw the notice about the bodies being found in the vault and just extrapolated, I mean, from where it is and everything—Sara had to have been murdered, why else would she be in there . . ."

"There you are," exclaimed Bewley. "I reckon Allsort sneaked in here yesterday and thumped that constable."

"No! Why would I do that?" Ryan slumped. Pagano grabbed his arm, spun him around, and dropped him onto the staircase with the same gesture he'd use to throw a bag of garbage into a dumpster.

Alasdair rounded on Bewley. "You were telling us no one was here who shouldn't have been."

"I can't be everywhere at once, can I now?"

"Here," Pagano said to Alasdair. "Ryan was late getting to Greyfriars, he was trying to make it up to me by giving me a good lead, okay?"

"Not okay," Alasdair replied. "Perhaps he was extrapolating the body was Sara's, aye, but why'd he go saying she was murdered? Either he was by way of being there at the time, or he's knowing someone who was."

D. S. Gordon pushed past the constable into the entrance hall. "Are you all right, Miss Fairbairn?"

"Yes. Yes I am, thanks."

"P.C., ah . . ."

"Wallace, sir."

"P.C. Wallace, you took the names of the bus driver and the other witnesses?"

"That I did, sir."

"Good. Bewley, what are you doing here?"

The man's face suffused with red. "I'm. Working. Here."

"Mr. Prasad's not paying you to be drinking up the stock," Alasdair murmured.

Bewley shot him another glare, but the evidence of his own eyes and breath supported Alasdair's observation.

Gordon focused on the odd couple by the staircase. "Who are you?"

"Jason Pagano, from 'Beyond the Edge'." His frown now annotated by a smolder in his dark eyes, Pagano stepped forward. His catcher's mitt of a hand engulfed Gordon's. "Tristan Ryan, my associate. You're an active copper, I take it? We have work that needs doing, we're filming at Lady Niddry's Drawing Room tonight, if we could just get on with filling out forms or anything else you're needing."

"I'd be obliged if you'd step outside and hail a taxi," Alasdair said to Wallace. "Jean, is that your book?"

Yeah. Oh yeah. Jean handed Bewley the mug and picked up Davis's book. She checked to make sure Pagano had returned her phone to her bag—yes, there it was—and zipped the zipper. She stood up. Her leg and ankle twinged, but her knees had solidified and the tiles on the floor didn't shimmy beneath her feet. *Good.*

"Sergeant." Alasdair took Gordon to the side and spoke quickly and urgently. Bewley, Allsort and Sara, Ryan and—well, the only person coming out of this afternoon unscathed was Pagano. Maybe.

"Thank you again," Jean told him.

The constable stuck his head through the door. "Here's a taxi. Step lively, it's stopping traffic."

"Got it?" Alasdair said to Gordon.

"Yes, sir," Gordon returned.

Good man, Jean thought. He's not wasting his breath

telling Alasdair he's not in charge of anything here . . . Alasdair's arm—her husband's arm, to have and to hold—wrapped her shoulders and guided her out onto the sidewalk.

Chapter Seventeen

Purring, Dougie settled down in Jean's lap and rubbed his head against her arm. Of course, she was wearing the thick fuzzy robe that always attracted his attentions, but she didn't have to be any more cynical than was really necessary. He was doing his best to make her feel better, that was all. Just like the other man of the house.

"No, really," she said into the phone. "I'm okay."

Miranda's voice was as soothing as Dougie's purr. "Soon I'll be sending you out with a life jacket or safety harness. Unless I should be keeping you in, it being Friday the Thirteenth."

"Enemy action happens no matter the date." *Enemy,* Jean thought. *I've made an enemy.*

"If you're feeling up to Vasudev's 'do this evening . . .'" Miranda let the sentence wave delicately in the wind.

"Oh, I'm not missing out on that, never fear."

"Good show, Jean. Keep your pecker up."

That expression always made Jean smile, and this time was no exception. "Thanks. Talk to you tomorrow." She switched off the phone and set it down just as Alasdair emerged from the kitchen.

He wore his own dressing gown and slippers—thank goodness for two bathrooms—and carried a steaming mug in each hand. "Here's your cocoa."

"Thanks. I just can't face any more tea, even though you make a great cuppa."

A hot shower had eased the tight lines and pallid complexion of the face looking back at her from the bathroom mirror. The robe and Dougie, Miranda and the rich hot chocolate, and above all the solid presence of Alasdair himself, settled her in the present. *Survived another one.*

She thought again what a dangerous job it was, asking questions. But then, as Tolkien wrote, It's a dangerous business going out your door. You step onto the road, and there's no knowing where you might be swept off to.

Like Scotland, and the arms of Alasdair Cameron.

He sat down close beside her, drank from his mug of tea, and turned his gaze to the window. He, too, was probably telling himself he used to be a complete brain all by himself. But neither of them had ever been a complete heart, not alone.

As though he heard her thought, he wrapped his free arm around her shoulders.

"I left a long and probably incoherent message for Michael and Rebecca," she told him. "Hugh we'll be seeing in a couple hours at Lady Niddry's."

"No need to be going there the night, if you'd rather rest."

"Are you kidding? Davis and Pagano are both going to be there. Miranda's going to be hanging on every pixel I can produce."

"What was Hugh saying? There's no such thing as bad publicity?"

"He was joking. Vasudev isn't, inviting the gasoline and the flame. And a witness with a notebook. Unless throwing Pagano and Davis at each other was Nicola's idea. Whatever, I bet I won't be the only media there."

"Nor I the only cop," Alasdair stated.

Look at that—beyond the window a rift in the overcast revealed a tiny strip of Prussian blue twilight. They could go back out without getting wet yet again. Jean wondered how long you had to live here before you starting growing lichen.

Alasdair's voice had the soft texture of moss. "The question is whether Pagano's Ryan'll be attending. I told Gordon he'd best be taking the lad in for further questioning. Well, Ryan's in his thirties, but still . . ."

"He seems younger than that."

"No matter. He knows more than he's telling."

"Oh yeah. He might be afraid of someone. Pagano? Or he's afraid of what will happen to him if he tells all. Or happen to someone else, even. Bewley really did seem surprised to see him, although I suppose it could be an elaborate act." She sipped a bit more chocolate therapy. "Bottom line: someone tried to kill me. Or at least tried to put me out of commission, and didn't mind if I was killed in the process."

"No one'd be chucking you beneath a bus if you weren't asking good questions, getting close to the truth of the matter."

"That's hardly comforting. Whatever happened to the good old anonymous phone call?"

"Even that was never making you back off."

"Or you." He raised his mug in acknowledgment. She went on, "Twice today, I thought someone was watching me. With the rain and everything, he—or she—saw their chance. Sort of like coshing poor P.C. Ross to get into the vault . . . Oh! I think I know what they were looking for!"

Alasdair listened intently while she explained about Robin Davis, the silver skull on his watch fob, the charms he'd given his favorites. "He was telling you he gave Sara one? Knox should be searching the scene again, then. Assuming the hand behind the cosh didn't find the skull and carry it away."

"Assuming there's something about that particular charm that would be a clue to whoever killed Sara. If all it has on it is her initials, that's not going to tell us very much. Whatever, you're not searching the scene again."

"No. I'm having me a posh dinner. And a show, it sounds like."

Jean's smile was lopsided. "Sara had a skull charm. Is it that big a leap to think that Nicola had one, too? Has one, tucked away somewhere?"

"Nicola. What were you saying, there at the Playfair Building, you were distracted and someone tripped you up because you were thinking about Nicola's middle initial?"

"Oh yeah." Jean leaned forward and Dougie opened a warning eye. Never mind—she could show Alasdair the card later. "She's Davis's publicist. He gave me one of her cards to give Miranda. N.C. MacLaren. What does that 'C' stand for?"

His brows lifted in comprehension. "Christine or the like?

Chris? Well then."

"When I asked Michael if he remembered someone named Chris, Rebecca asked whether it was a man or a woman. They hadn't heard Amy say boyfriend. I had. I told them it was a man. But . . ."

" . . . Amy was saying their parents were conservative sorts. She was saying their dad was thinking he'd failed with Sara . . ."

". . . she said Sara was trying out all sorts of, well, lifestyles. Why not a girlfriend? And a fling with the American in the group as well, I guess. Funny. Poor Grizel Hamilton was called immoral. Sara's father called her immoral. And there they were in the vault, together, neither of them at all immoral by today's standards."

Alasdair gazed toward the window, where the clouds might be thinning but the sun was also setting, eliminating any chance of actual light. "Gordon was telling me that he visited P.C. Ross this morning, who looks to be making a full recovery . . ."

"Thank goodness."

". . . but he's still right muzzy, mumbling about Nicola in her window across the street."

"She made quite an impression on him. But that's how she works, making an impression. What if she came into the Playfair Building with some story for him about, oh, things stored in the cellar? He'd escort her down there, and wham! I know Bewley said no one had been who shouldn't have been there . . ."

". . . likely meaning he saw no strangers."

"But then he also said he couldn't be everywhere and see everything."

"I'd not be taking his word on the time of day," stated Alasdair.

"Me neither." In her lap, Dougie was no longer purring but snoring, radiating the oblivion of sleep. Jean yawned, then told herself, *not yet*. "Maybe Nicola was angry at Bewley yesterday morning, when Ross saw her telling him off, because he'd opened up the door and she knew what was in the vault and that she might be compromised somehow. I mean, she's got a public relations job, she's managing Pippa's—and that place is neat as a pin, you should see it . . ."

"You stopped by the shop?" He wasn't smiling. That wasn't a flirtatious question. A slight sheen of ice formed on his expression, the sort that the unwary skater could fall through.

Oh for the love of . . . "I had a few minutes between checking out the site of the theater and talking to Davis, so I thought I'd ask her a few questions—good grief, I never told you about the theater, either, the Hamiltons' cave and everything . . ."

"Going behind Knox's back, were you, questioning suspects?"

"Nicola wasn't anything more than a casual witness then, not a suspect. Besides, you were the one who suggested I talk to Davis."

"You've got a legitimate interest in him, with his book and all."

"You went behind Knox's back with Amy."

"She phoned me," he snapped, and, a second too late, amended, "She phoned us."

Dougie stirred and opened an eye. *Now children* . . . "Don't worry," Jean said stiffly, "Nicola blew me off. I have nothing to report to Knox. All that happened was I roused somebody's suspicions and almost got killed."

She hadn't meant that to come out the way it had, but Alasdair winced, cracking the sheen of ice. His eyes warmed to the color of the North Atlantic. "Sorry."

"So am I. It's just that . . ."

"I know. And Nicola wasn't telling Knox anything either. It's all circumstantial, but still, time Knox was having another go at her. And getting a warrant and searching her flat and her office. As for Davis . . ."

"He might be the mover and shaker behind it all, but I sure didn't turn anything up that Knox would find actionable. On the other hand, I think found where the second entrance to the vault is. Or was." Jean went on with all the details she could remember—and she didn't think the bus had knocked any out of her mind. At last, with a parting squeeze of Jean's shoulders, Alasdair drained his mug and headed for phone.

She was never going to take the policeman out of the spouse, Jean told herself. Not that she really wanted to.

Dougie was now sprawled in her lap, paws flopping. "Sorry, little guy. Places to go, and so forth." She started shoving him onto the couch. He half-opened his eyes, but otherwise didn't move a muscle. How a cat the size of a loaf of bread could make itself weigh the equivalent of, well, a sack of cement, was yet another mystery of physics.

From the bedroom window Jean looked out toward the castle, now no more than a hulking mass dotted by a lamp or two. That eerie gray-green glow in the clouds over the topmost tower must be the moon following the sun into the west. The esplanade was as dark as it would ever get in the midst of a modern city. If any ghosts walked through the mingled light and shadow, they walked alone.

Jean applied make-up and was glad to see her complexion was no longer the color of chalk. Her stomach was back to normal, too—it growled piteously as she pulled on her red New Year's Eve dress.

Red. The color of Valentine's Day, of love, of passion. Of a matador's cape brandished before a bull. *Come and get me.* Jean supposed she was no less a target than Alasdair, but she'd already proved she was easier to get the drop on.

It wasn't, she told herself, that she was getting used to this sort of adventure, it was that her adventures had shaved so many fibers off her nervous system she no longer had as many to get excited. Still she ached all over, and several of the roses in her cheeks were evidence of a rising anger at the gall of whoever had taken her one and only life into his own hands.

By the time Alasdair appeared in the bedroom, Jean was sitting on the edge of the bed leafing through Davis's battered book.

He laid his phone on the dresser. "Right. Thanks to public records, Knox had it at her fingertips within a minute's time. Nicola Christine MacLaren. Born in Stornoway, Isle of Lewis."

"Stornoway? She's quite a glamour girl to come from a

dour place like Stornoway."

"Everyone's coming from somewhere. She's been cutting a swathe here in the big city a long time since."

"Has she ever."

"We're still needing confirmation that she's Sara's Chris, though."

"And where does Ryan come in?"

"From stage left, like as not." He dived into the wardrobe. "Is that Davis's book? How'd that part of the interview go, over and beyond the bits about the skull charms and Nicola C. and all."

"Davis is a smug so-and-so. He seems to have no problem making pets of his female students, thinks they're lucky to have him. I'd almost like to find out he murdered Sara, just to bring him down a peg or two."

Alasdair emerged with his kilt and Argyll jacket. "You're disagreeing with his paranormal-is-bunk theory, are you?"

"Of course I am. You and I both know that ghosts exist, however you want to define them. Still, I don't so much disagree with his premise as with his attitude. You have to have premises."

"Oh aye. We're needing a place to live, right enough." Alasdair vanished into the bathroom before she could throw anything at him.

Laughing, she opened the book to the index and scanned the listed topics. Despite her irritation with Davis, she also had a mote of sympathy for him. Academic infighting made your average Tudor court look like a love-in. It was survival not of the fittest but of the boldest . . .

Her eye stopped at the m's. "Mortsafe". *Okay*. She flipped to the page, and, as a bekilted Alasdair stepped back out of the bathroom threading his sporran onto his belt, she read aloud, "The mortsafe is an example of how the human mind seizes upon primitive fears. There is much greater public utility in studying the human body than in hiding it away and using it as the bogeyman in children's fairy tales. Burke and Hare, for example, were turned into murderers by such fears. The motive of Doctor Robert Knox was of the best: the advancement of human knowledge."

"Right." Alasdair settled the belt around his kilt. "I'm thinking Burke and Hare had freedom of will. Barely a pot to piss in, granted, but freedom of will."

Jean closed the book. "To turn his own metaphor around, you can put all the iron bars around yourself that you want, you can lock your body and your brain into a cage, but you're still confronted with the inexplicable. If you want to believe, you'll do it on the slightest of evidence. If you want to disbelieve, ditto. There's more than just freedom of will at work there. There's freedom of imagination, too."

Alasdair leaned closer to the full-length mirror on the back of the closet door, tying his green tie that complemented the secondary color in his mostly red Cameron tartan kilt. Scarlet red, unlike her crimson red dress. Both the color of blood. Fresh blood, pumping away in her body and his as well.

"Although if you were protecting your mind, your sensibilities," she said, "you wouldn't call it a mortsafe. You'd call it an anima safe. A vita safe . . . No, that sounds too much like a food supplement."

He slipped on his jacket. "Good to see you're back in form, Jean."

"Thank you, Alasdair." She considered the mustard-yellow dust jacket of the book, now torn to reveal the navy blue binding beneath. A rip ran diagonally through the etching of the man and the stage-ghost.

"Ghosts for Fun and Profit" had presumably featured ghosts on wires. And what else? Did the real, as distinct from metaphorical, mortsafe come into it at all—and she didn't mean Billy's aluminum-foil replica. What about the bones of Ranald Hamilton, which had been moved by someone who'd been working with glitter?

Had Davis been pushing envelopes and cutting edges with his show, or had he been robbing a grave?

Alasdair stood before her, hand extended. "Shall we?"

Her gaze settled on the leather straps and buckles securing

the sides of his kilt. Now there was erotic gear, never mind what Nicola intended for the buckles and straps in her shop. She should have retorted to Alasdair's earlier charge that she had a legitimate reason to visit Pippa's Erotic Gear as well as one to interview Davis.

Smiling, she popped up and took Alasdair's hand, and was closing in further when, from her evening bag on the dresser, came an electronic version of "The Campbells are Coming". "Ah, Michael." With a peck on Alasdair's shaving-cream scented cheek, Jean answered the phone.

"You're all right, then?" asked Rebecca's voice.

"Oh yeah. Once again I'm living to tell the tale."

"If someone's trying to push you under a bus, you must be closing in on solving the case."

"It's easier to pick on me than on a six-foot-tall redheaded police detective."

A wail rose in the background, accompanied by a soothing paternal murmur. "Sorry," Rebecca said. "The wee bairnie's hungry. I just wanted to check in and pass on something from Michael. He's been racking his brain . . ."

"There's an image for you," Jean said, tilting the phone so Alasdair could hear as well. Funny how bodies and body parts were rather on her mind at the moment.

" . . . about people he knew back in the old days, and he thinks there was a lass, not a lad, named Chrissie hanging about The Body Snatcher. Not one you'd notice, he's saying, plain, dowdy, kind of shadowing the other girls. I know you're looking for a boy . . ."

"Not any more," Jean told her. "Now we *are* looking for a girl. Michael's description doesn't fit, but that was fifteen years ago. You can do a lot with cosmetics in fifteen years."

"And he's saying that when the police are done with that mortsafe, to have them contact the Museum. That's something that could be displayed alongside all the other peculiar—and I do mean peculiar, in some cases—Scottish artifacts." Linda shrieked. "Gotta run. Good luck. Enjoy your posh evening out."

"Thanks." Jean switched off the phone and tucked it away.

Beside her, Alasdair's mouth settled into a grim line. "I'm not thinking enjoyment's quite the intention, not now."

Chapter Eighteen

Jean walked the few paces from the taxi to the portico of Lady Niddry's trying not to look over her shoulder. She had Alasdair beside her now. And that tall woman just stepping into the lobby was D. I. Wendy Knox, dressed in an elegant pants suit, teal blue satin blouse, and diamond earrings.

If Jean didn't know better, she'd have thought the slight figure beside Knox was the dummy to her ventriloquist. They even had similar red hair, although his was more orange and less spiky. So Ryan was here after all, if under escort. Knox couldn't resist having all her persons of interest under one roof.

Inside the door, Jean had to look twice to make sure she'd come to the same place she'd visited that morning. Now the chandelier blazed and the black-and-white tile floor swirled with at least thirty other guests. White-jacketed servitors took coats and offered snacks and drinks. The doors to one side stood open on a drawing room that George III and Queen Charlotte—or the restorers of Colonial Williamsburg—would have recognized, right down to the blue walls and lavish Turkey carpet. Servers were spreading an ornately carved buffet with an array of delicacies. Red and white flowers lavished every surface. Either an invisible string quartet or a CD played something classical.

No, Alasdair wasn't the only man there wearing a kilt— although he was without doubt, Jean thought, the handsomest. Nor, as she'd suspected, was she the only member of the fourth estate in attendance. She recognized at least one print and one television reporter taking in the scene as well as the food and drink.

Here came a waiter balancing a silver tray loaded with champagne flutes. Alasdair took two and handed one to Jean. She did no more than sip—bubbly goodness wasn't so good on an empty stomach. But another waiter approached with a tray of hors d'oeuvres. She appropriated a cheesy bit and a tiny meat pie and only then met the beady brown eyes of the server. Des Bewley.

He looked odd with neither his hard hat nor his stubble, as though the whiskers had migrated upwards to form a fuzz over his cranium. For once he exuded an aroma of mouthwash rather than beer or whisky or both, and for once he was smiling, if stiffly, the expression glued on. But his eyes were still bloodshot, as though he hadn't slept since he'd unblocked that door and, like opening Pandora's Box, released the contents of the vault.

"Oh. Hi," Jean said. "Moonlighting here, are you?"

"Chap called in sick, and herself threw me into his monkey suit. Another few quid's all to the good, eh?"

"Yes, it is," Jean told him, and he moved on through the crowd.

Knox was telling Alasdair, ". . . Ryan's refusing to tell us much more than he's already told us, though, thanks to your new information, he's admitted he had a rival for Sara's affections, a woman named Chrissie. And he doesn't know what's become of her. He's saying he wasn't telling us, not wanting to speak ill of the dead."

"No one's getting exercised over a same-sex relationship," said Alasdair. "Well, save Sara's own father."

"But was the girl known as Chrissie then, the same woman known as Nicola now?" Jean looked up the elegant curving staircase. Now the door to Pippa's was shut, and the pink sign was dark, even though she could still make out the letters.

Jason Pagano had set up shop in the shadowed area beneath the stairs. He was still dressed in black, a suit cut to fit his muscular frame, a black shirt with the sheen of silk, and a black bolo tie. His police leash at its maximum length, Ryan accepted his computer tablet from Jason's hand. Beside him, Liz Estrada wore a Jane Austen-style high-waisted dress, her dark hair lying over her shoulders in sausage-like ringlets. Was she impersonating the resident ghost? If so, her clothing was no more than a wild guess based on the age of the building.

"Ryan worked here when it was a student meeting-place," Knox went on. "Recently he heard some tale about a ghost. He thought it must be Sara's. Nothing like a guilty conscience to produce bogles in the shadows."

"A guilty conscience is likely enough, aye, but he's still keeping his head down," said Alasdair. "And Gordon's back in the vault, you're saying?"

"With two constables, a magnifying glass, and a fine tooth comb. I'm telling him to come back with that skull charm or he needn't come back at all." Knox's smile smacked of dry satisfaction, as though she was contrasting her congenial surroundings with Gordon's.

Did he deserve the hard time she was giving him, Jean wondered? What did he do, make some bad jokes at her expense? Surely he hadn't made a pass at her, although he might have hit on someone else.

Alasdair, of course, was sticking to business. "What if the person who hit Ross already found the charm?"

"We're searching the bar," Knox replied, "especially Bewley's office, and his flat."

"Bewley's? Not Nicola MacLaren's?"

"Hers as well, since she's giving Bewley his orders. But then, you'll not have heard yet. Ross's head is clearing. He's saying he's never shared two words with MacLaren. He was keeping watch, heard someone on the stairs, and next thing he knew, lights out."

"You're still thinking it was Bewley, then."

"I am that."

Jean snagged a puff pastry from a passing tray, dared a good swallow of her champagne, and said, "You do know that Bewley's here, right?"

Knox spun around. "Eh?"

"Nicola put him to work in place of a waiter who called in sick."

"And you know that how?"

"He told me, when I took a snack off his tray five minutes

ago." Jean bit into the pastry. Spicy green stuff. Peas? Spinach? Whatever.

Behind Knox's back Alasdair sent Jean a quick grin.

The front door opened. Amy Herries walked in, on the arm of a man Jean recognized as one of her work-in-laws at *The Scotsman*. Jean would have thought Amy was dressed to the nines, except her outfit was so abbreviated she was more dressed to the sixes. Catching her eye, Jean smiled.

Amy's black-lined eyes and red lips returned the smile, if a bit shamefacedly. As the couple walked past, she leaned in and whispered, "I'm wanting a good look at Robin Davis. I'm thinking my sister would still be alive, but for him."

Jean had no good answer to that, so contented herself with a nod at Amy and another at the *Scotsman* stringer. Who had approached whom, she wondered. The victim's sister's story in exchange for entry to the party.

Vasudev made his entrance from a door at the back of the lobby next to the cloak room. His dinner jacket fit perfectly, his shoes shone like mirrors, his moustache curled and his hair waved just so. "Good to see you, welcome, glad you could join us . . ." He worked his way through the room, pressing flesh and air-kissing.

And here came Davis himself through the front door, looking less like Winnie-the-Pooh than Dracula, all tuxedo, tie, and teeth. At his side walked a woman even younger than Amy, in a dress even skimpier, exposing legs as long as a politician's nose that ended in thick-soled, high-heeled shoes.

Jean asked herself when she'd stumbled into middle age, one-inch block heels and all. Then she saw the silver skull dangling on a fine chain at the girl's neck. Davis was still up to his tricks.

"Ah, Jean, good to see you," he said, leaning in to kiss her.

She dodged, flipping her hand up into his. "Nice to see you again, too. May I introduce my husband, Alasdair Cameron?"

Alasdair and Davis exchanged handshakes and polite mutters, and the girl's name and giggle came and went, but

Davis's eye had spotted Pagano and his crew at the foot of the staircase, Liz poised on the bottom tread. Brushing by Knox without even glancing at her, Davis plunged through the crowd with his date tripping along behind. Almost literally—a man in a kilt grabbed her arm and steadied her on her shoes.

Pagano looked around. "Well, well, well. If it's not the professor of denial."

"If it's not public charlatan number one," replied Davis.

The crowd eddied, forming a semi-circle with Vasudev at one wing. A few cell phones rose like periscopes, cameras clicking. Ryan looked up from his computer and made arcane gestures at two men toting camera and sound equipment. The recording devices leaned in. A bright light flared. Pagano's shadow rushed up the wall.

Knox crossed her arms quizzically. Vasudev stood with his hands folded behind his back, head tilted to the side, moustache shading a gleaming smile.

Pagano raised a blinking electronic device in each hand, not unlike a priest with his cross and his holy water. But instead of thrusting them into Davis's face, he turned to the camera. "A ghost walks Lady Niddry's Drawing Room. It's a woman, they say. But this fine-dining establishment is set in one of the most haunted parts of Edinburgh, the South Bridge, known to be the haunt of the Mackenzie Poltergeist."

Pagano inspected his gadgets. "We're getting a fluctuation in the magnetic field. There's definitely something here."

Liz ran up the stairs, struck a pose, ran down again. Overhead, the chandelier started to swing back and forth. The crowd gasped, glasses clinked, and people backed away. Exchanging a puzzled glance with Alasdair, Jean thought of the chandelier scenario from *The Phantom of the Opera*—but that took place in the Paris catacombs, not Edinburgh's, a detail a showman like Pagano would never miss.

A noise percolated into her awareness. The ticking of a distant clock? No. Robin Davis tut-tutting as loudly as he could. Heads turned away from Pagano and toward him. "Rubbish! There's a fishing line attached to the chandelier. See, it's catching the light."

Everyone looked up. The chandelier slowly stopped swaying. Knox nodded. "Looks to be a line, yes."

"That's a cobweb," stated Pagano.

A familiar voice said, "There'll be no cobwebs in any establishment under my management, thank you just the same."

On cue, everyone turned toward the drawing room. Nicola stood in the doorway. Her black sheath dress, cut down to here and slit up to there, gleamed like the scales of a snake and fit just as snugly. Red jewels shone at her throat and in her ears beneath her upswept hair, matching the red of her lipstick.

She waved one arm in a graceful movement worthy of *Swan Lake*. "Ladies and gentlemen, please enjoy our hors d'oeuvres buffet before taking your places in our dining room downstairs."

And what, Jean asked herself as everyone surged toward the drawing room, did you call a female maitre d'? A maitresse d'? Now that did sound like a dominatrix.

Amy hung back, eyeing Davis and his companion, who still stood beneath the chandelier. Finally she allowed her own companion to sweep her away. The lobby almost cleared, Davis called to Pagano, "There's proof for you, that ghosts and poltergeists are no more than the products of a diseased mind."

"There's proof for you," Pagano replied, "that diseased minds are the ones closed to the evil forces walking the Earth."

"Evil forces inhabit human bodies, not old buildings," said Knox, half to herself.

"Disproving Pagano," commented Alasdair beside Jean, "doesn't disprove the paranormal."

"And vice versa."

Knox stepped forward as though to mediate. Vasudev looked over his shoulder, brow furrowed—he'd miscalculated how strongly the buffet would attract all the reporters. *No such thing as bad publicity . . .*

The breath went out of Jean's chest as though she'd been punched in the stomach. Her shoulders slumped beneath the cold burden of the paranormal. Pagano and Davis's rising voices faded to a buzz. Laboriously, she stepped to the side, bumping her shoulder against Alasdair's. She felt the slow, viscous shudder tracing its way through his own body. As one, they looked up.

On the landing of the staircase stood the ghost of Grizel Hamilton.

Chapter Nineteen

Grizel stood in the landing, rather, the hem of her dress not just brushing the planks of the floor, but mingling with them. The banisters below the railing sketched black verticals against the soft gray-white of her apron. Her hands were folded in front of her chest, her downcast eyes half-hidden by the rim of her bonnet.

"That's how she was standing when Gordon and I . . ." Alasdair began in a hoarse whisper.

Suddenly Grizel lurched forward and fell. No, suddenly she was pushed over the edge, Jean corrected. The railing passed through her body. The staircase and Pagano's crew, Davis and Knox, all became momentary shadows through it, as though through a fog. Then Grizel hit the floor and lay motionless, twisted, one stockinged foot—the shoe must have gone flying at impact—emerging piteously from her skirts.

The face beneath the bonnet was still calm, still quiet. Jean was as sure as she'd ever been of anything that the open eyes were far from sightless. They searched for another world, a distant horizon just beyond reach . . .

The apparition vanished. The cold eased, the weight lifted. Alasdair's shoulder rose and fell in a breath like the one Jean took. Flowers. Perfume. Food.

Gesturing in frustration, Ryan walked across the patch of floor—just black and white tiles, no bloodstains—where Grizel had lain and headed for the drawing room. Making a precise about-face, Knox followed. "Mr. Ryan."

"Yeah," he said over his shoulder.

"The woman in the doorway, Nicola MacLaren. Was that Sara's Chrissie?"

"No way. Chrissie was, well, just a girl . . ." They disappeared through the doorway.

Rats, Jean thought.

Exchanging sneers rather than the names of seconds, Davis grabbed his arm candy and Pagano gathered his troops, and they, too, moved off.

Alasdair shook his head. "That was never Sara Herries."

"Nope. It was Grizel, still walking buildings that didn't exist when she was alive. More like a guardian angel than a haunting ghost."

"Not a ghost of Pagano's sort, at the least."

Vasudev was frowning up at the chandelier. Jean followed his gaze. The almost transparent filament swaying in a slight draft was definitely fishing line. Someone had thrown one end over a curving brass arm, then looped the other around one of the banisters along the staircase. When Liz ran up the steps, she'd used her toe to give the line a pull.

"I'd have expected something a wee bit more sophisticated from Pagano," said Alasdair.

"Spur of the moment, I bet," Jean returned.

Sighing heavily, Vasudev stepped forward. "Jean, Mr. Cameron—I beg your pardon, I never introduced myself properly, Vasudev Prasad—if you'd be so kind as to come downstairs with me, ahead of the rest of our guests, I, well, I have a confession to make." Without waiting for a reply, he walked off into the drawing room.

"Confession?" Jean asked faintly, just as Alasdair said, "Right."

Side by side, they followed Vasudev through the open doorway. There was Bewley again. Alasdair took the opportunity to leave their empty glasses with him—his tray was now empty and, Jean noted, his breath was no longer minty fresh.

There was Pagano, chatting up Nicola, who offered him a slow smile. There was Davis preening and handing out cards or bookmarks. There was Knox, her phone to her ear, and Ryan beside her looking like a dishrag that had been wrung out and hung up to dry.

Vasudev opened one of another set of double doors and motioned Jean and Alasdair through. With a glance at the faces turning their way—who were they to merit special treatment?—Jean stepped through and stopped dead, Alasdair piling up behind her.

She stood on a spacious part-landing, part-balcony overlooking a vast underground space that was to the vault below the Playfair Building what St. Giles Cathedral was to a Covenanter's cave. The stone walls were scrubbed clean and supported myriad small candles, making the room swim in a golden glow. The arched ceiling receded into the distance— aha, there at the far end were Hugh and Billy and the others, setting up on a stage under hidden electric lights. Between the door and the stage, servers tweaked crystal, silver, and red roses atop linen-draped tables. *Cool!* While Jean would have preferred a room with a view, this space was open enough to work for her.

Alasdair stepped up to Jean's right and Vasudev to her left. "This was a double-height vault to begin with," the owner said. "During renovations, we had the original stone flags flooring the vault removed. That exposed the medieval alley or wynd beneath, and the foundations of the houses on either side. We shifted the rubble, evened the floors, filled potholes with an acrylic substance, all to make a safe walking surface. Now our guests can dine on the finest twenty-first century cuisine while seated in structures hundreds of years old. Please go on down."

Jean passed a swinging door that no doubt led into the kitchens, and went on down first one flight of stairs, then, doubling back at a landing, a second. Her hand ran lightly along an elegant wrought-iron railing no original dweller in the vaults would have recognized. Arriving on the clear surface topping a medieval cobblestoned street, she tried not to think about the archaeological knowledge destroyed by the renovations. Like ghosts, Edinburgh had a surfeit of archaeology.

Hugh waved. Beside him, Billy looked up from some arcane operation on his pipes and his rawboned face lit with recognition. He beckoned. She made a just-a-minute gesture and turned back to Vasudev. *Confession?*

Vasudev's dark brown eyes moved from Jean's inquisitive

expression to Alasdair's impassive one and back again. "I was not quite forthcoming with you and Miranda yesterday morning. Jason Pagano did not ring me and ask for permission to film here. I heard he was planning a program here in Edinburgh and I rang him—well, I actually spoke with his assistant, Tristan Ryan—and told him the tale of the ghost on the staircase in the entrance hall. I was hoping the popularity of his work would translate into customers for Lady Niddry's."

Aha, Jean thought. "Do you know the name of the waiter who says he saw the ghost to begin with?"

"No. He's long gone. I never spoke with him myself. The story is no more than a rumor amongst the staff, one intended to frightened the newcomer, I expect. In any event, I only meant it as a lure for Mr. Pagano. I sweetened the deal by offering an unopened vault, the one beneath the Playfair Building."

Alasdair nodded. "The vault turned out to be holding an even greater attraction."

"It was, yes." Vasudev grimaced. "Please understand, I had no intention of opening up a very recent missing-persons case along with the vault. If I'd known this would mean injury to a policeman and to yourself, Jean, I'd never have pursued the matter. I must ask your forgiveness."

"Well, I, ah," she stammered, thinking that *no problem* was too blatant a white lie. And asking what Vasudev's silent and exceedingly circumspect partner, Miranda's Duncan Kerr, thought of all this was too blatant a question. "I know you didn't mean anything bad to happen."

Vasudev bowed in acknowledgment. "We do go a bit overboard with our marketing schemes, don't we?"

Nicola appeared on the landing two stories above and peered over the railing. Now there, Jean told herself, was a "we".

Alasdair, too, gazed up at Nicola, a still figure at the fulcrum of two columns of servers marching up and down the stairs like ants. He lowered his gaze to the array of candles, the multiple flicker reflecting in his eyes. February, thought Jean.

Not Ground Hog Day but Candlemas, the Christian gloss on an old Celtic fire festival closing out the darkest time of the year. Valentine's Day, buds bursting into bloom, shoppers at Pippa's Erotic Gear.

Of course Alasdair's train of thought pulled into a different station entirely. "Mr. Prasad, I understand you also own the Cowgate Bake Shop."

"Why yes. Duncan and I own quite a few properties in the area. I'm not sure the Bake Shop is quite up to Protect and Survive's standards, however."

One of Alasdair's brows quirked. *Oh.* Smoothly, he switched from policeman to head of P&S. "It was once a historic property, though. The Deacon's Throat . . ."

"Neck," Jean murmured.

" . . . Neck Theater. Wasn't that damaged in the 2002 fire?"

"Yes, sadly, it was. The front part of the building was a total loss, but what had been the backstage areas were still standing, if as little more than a shell. They abut the hillside there, mind you, which protected them."

"But I imagine there was a good deal of smoke damage, still."

"So there was. Witnesses tell me smoke was even eddying from the back of the building, hillside or no hillside. Strange the way smoke will behave, isn't it?"

"Very strange." Alasdair's glance at Jean added, *Strange the way smoke will go leaking even through hidden passages and sealed doorways, eh?*

"May I show you an interesting feature of the upper landing?" Vasudev asked. "We re-used original materials as best we could, and I believe we found mason's marks dating back to William Playfair's day."

"Of course." Alasdair nodded toward Billy—*carry on, Jean*—and followed Vasudev back up one set of steps just as Nicola ushered two waiters carrying wine chillers down the other.

Jean nipped down the room to the stage. Donnie's fingers

drew a trill from the keyboard, Jamie set down his guitar and thumped on his bodhran, Hugh tightened a fiddle string, and Billy produced a squeal from his pipes that had half the people in the room looking around in alarm—someone had undoubtedly stepped on a cat's tail.

Jean leaned across the bank of lights and speakers. "Billy?"

"Oh aye, Jean, that stunner coming down the stairs, wearing the black glove . . ."

Every one of eight male eyeballs turned to Nicola. She halted on the landing and consulted what had to be a PDA, although where she was keeping it in that outfit, Jean couldn't imagine.

". . . she was bringing us down here," Billy went on, "having us fed, making sure we were properly lubricated . . ."

Hugh indicated an empty glass that, judging by the foam remaining around its edge, had contained beer. "Fine local brew, mind you. They do things up properly here."

Billy angled closer to Jean. The long drones bundled beneath his arm clattered together like dry bones. "She was a friend of Sara Herries'. Plain little thing then, brown hair, but quick, very quick. I was half an hour identifying her just now."

Whoa. No wonder Ryan didn't recognize her. "She was Chrissie then?" Jean asked.

"Never knew her name. What I'm minding is the row she was having with Sara, the afternoon of the night Sara went missing. Something about Robin Davis, something about jealousy."

"They were arguing in the theater?"

"Oh aye. Back behind the stage whilst they were pasting glitter and glam on the scenery. They saw me coming and shut up right smart."

"Thank you, Billy. That's really helpful."

"We're aiming to please," Hugh said and turned to the band. "'The Mucking of Geordie's Byre,' lads. One, two . . ." The cheerful music rang out.

Jean started back down the length of the floor. That tune seemed appropriate, considering how the gutters of the old wynd would once have smelled, in the days when waste disposal meant emptying chamber pots out the window. If passersby were lucky, they'd get a shout of warning.

Jean hurried up the right-hand steps and arrived on the balcony just as Ryan did, too, propelled from behind by Knox. Jean went so far as to pluck at Knox's sleeve, pulling her ear closer. "Billy Skelton," she whispered. "He's identified Nicola as Sara's friend, said he heard them having a major argument the same day Sara went missing."

"All right then," replied Knox, *thank you* apparently being superfluous, and again directed Ryan's attention to Nicola. "Have yourself a long look."

He glanced at her, then, in a double-take, had himself a long look. Astonishment filled his face and he spun back to Knox. "Chrissie. It is her. Damn. Who'd have thought?"

A waiter carrying several wine glasses walked past them, then stopped behind Vasudev and Alasdair. Bewley again.

Ryan went on, "Okay, you've got your ID, my team's moving the equipment in here, I need to . . ."

". . . be helping them by setting up another trick?" Knox asked.

"No, no, I slipped that guy Bewley five pounds to fix the chandelier, thought it would help. Amateur effort, though."

He didn't realize, Jean told herself, that Bewley was standing right there, listening. Scowling. By the angle of her head and the glint in her eye, Knox did.

Alasdair and Vasudev inspected a stone block set into the floor by the balcony railing. That is, Vasudev pointed to the block and spoke. Alasdair might have been standing over it, but Jean could tell by his body language he was listening to Knox play with her suspect like a cat with a mouse.

Nicola swanned by them all as if they didn't exist and opened the other half of the double doors into the drawing room.

"You're quite sure you never met Bewley in your student days here?" Knox asked Ryan.

"I've told you again and again, there were lots of people

hanging around back then."

"And was there a row between Sara and Chrissie, the night she went missing?"

Ryan went so pale the color seemed to fade even from his hair. He took a step toward the door. Knox's hand on his arm drew him back. Another waiter—funny, he looked familiar, too—slipped by. This is the stage, Jean thought, not down there where the lads were playing.

Nicola stiffened and turned slowly toward Knox. In the doorway loomed a black thundercloud with a white dress at its side. Pagano and the inappropriately dressed—to be the house ghost, anyway—Liz. On his other side, Amy Herries pushed forward.

"I've just had a word with Sergeant Gordon," Knox told Nicola. "One of our constable's found a wee silver skull with the initials SAH in your flat, in your jewelry box. Sara Anne Herries, I'm thinking."

"I knew her," Nicola said coolly. "We were both Robin's students. I kept a memento."

Now Davis himself was peering through the doorway, his companion forming a buffer between him and Pagano. Knox's forefinger targeted the skull at the girl's throat. "Gordon's found an identical one in the vault, black with tarnish, looking to be a bit of gravel next the mortsafe. This one's got the initials NCM. Nicola Christine MacLaren."

Nicola's cheeks went from porcelain to pasty. Without blinking, her gaze switched from Knox's face to Ryan's. Ryan stared at her, slowly shaking his head, his lips forming the words, "I never told anyone. I swear, I never told anyone."

Bewley took a step back, toward Alasdair and Vasudev, the glasses in his hand clinking. Alasdair spun around.

Knox focused on Bewley, her smile utterly without humor. "And you there, Bewley. One of my colleagues has been interviewing the folk gathered at the bus stop outside the Playfair Building this afternoon. You were seen stepping out and walking up the street, then joining the queue waiting for the bus, the queue that collapsed into a scrum soon as the bus came along. Tired of working, were you? Wandering about the neighborhood? Thinking of going home early? Or were you keeping an eye on Miss Fairbairn here, thought maybe she was asking a few too many questions?"

Jean's nervous system dripped ice water. That's who she'd seen looking at her from the South Bridge, and later through the window of the coffee bar as she talked to Davis. That's who had tripped her up.

"I'm hearing from the hospital as well. Your old chum Constable Ross is growing positively coherent, is saying the last thing he's remembering before being knocked unconscious is the smell of drink. I've never spoken with you that you didn't reek of it."

"Damn you," Bewley said. "Damn you all."

"Here," said Vasudev, stepping forward, perhaps to remonstrate, perhaps to stop the scene until all the reporters could watch.

Alasdair blocked him with an outstretched arm. "Bewley . . ."

In the instant Alasdair moved, so did Bewley. He dropped every glass but one. The sound of smashing crystal blanked out that of the band. Leaping forward, he swept Alasdair back and halfway over the railing. The remaining glass cracked against the iron and Bewley was holding a shard like a small dagger against Alasdair's throat.

Time stopped. Jean saw the glittering sharpness press against the fair skin. She saw the blood well up and trickle down into the white collar. She saw Alasdair's face, very still. She saw one of his hands grasping the railing, white-knuckled, pushing back—a inch further and he'd fall two stories onto a stone floor—his other hand rose slowly behind Bewley's arm. The shard cut deeper.

A woman screamed. No, Jean realized, it wasn't her. She wasn't even breathing. Her heart was a lead weight in her chest. It must have been Liz. Screaming was her specialty. Unless it had been Amy.

Davis's voice—it had to be Davis—said reverently, "Oh

my God."

Knox's voice was acid-etched contempt. "What's the good of this, Bewley?"

Alasdair's blood was the color of the red squares in his tartan. He was dressed to kill, Jean's mind shouted, not to die.

"Bewley, you're making matters worse."

The music died away, echoing down the vault. Vasudev's rich brown skin turned gray. Knox was gathering herself for a leap—no, no, he'll cut Alasdair's carotid artery—other bodies were pressing forward . . .

"Des, you poor sod," said Nicola's modulated tones. "If you'd only kept quiet. If you'd only left well alone. Let the man go. It's too late now."

A curt if infinitesimal nod from Knox, and the waiter who looked familiar—oh, P.C. Wallace, of course Knox would have back-up—discorporated and reappeared with his arm around Bewley's throat. He jerked him backward. Pagano grabbed Bewley's arm just as Alasdair pushed it away. Knox herself twisted his wrist until the glass fell to the floor and shattered.

Jean's feet didn't touch the balcony, didn't crunch on the broken glass. She flew to Alasdair's side and pulled him upright, away from the railing, away from the drop. Great, now she was going to be acrophobic, too.

His arm wrapped her waist so firmly her bones creaked. With a shaky exhalation, he accepted a starched white handkerchief from Vasudev and pressed it to his throat. "I'm all right, Jean."

Lights flickered—oh, all the periscope-like cell phones were extended again, getting the scoop.

Pagano and Wallace held Bewley between them. Knox grasped him by his lapels and leaned in. "Des Bewley, I arrest you for . . ."

"No!" someone shouted.

Jean looked around. So did Alasdair. Everyone froze.

Tristan Ryan stepped forward. "I did it."

"Did what?" asked Knox.

"I murdered Sara Herries. It was me. I did it."

Chapter Twenty

Having obtained Knox's permission to carry on with his plans, Vasudev had organized his guests into the dining room downstairs, ordered the servers to begin bringing out the food, and asked Hugh to create music. Now the chime of intact glassware and the clink of silver applied to china filtered up into the drawing room, and the chatter of voices discussing the evening's exciting events rose and fell. Jean imagined Pagano holding court on one side of the vault while Davis handed out plastic glow-in-the-dark skulls on the other.

Each had had his moment with Knox. Each would no doubt be chagrined to know how much his replies had sounded like the other's: Who me? I know nothing.

She'd waved Pagano away, and scheduled Davis to make a formal statement avowing that he was the most innocent of bystanders and mild-mannered of ivory-tower inhabitants, and just how, please, should he have known that his colleague Nicola had once answered to her middle name?

Now Hugh was carrying out his promise to play Burns's "A Man's a Man for All That". Jean mouthed the words: *What though on hamely fare we dine, Wear hoddin grey, an' a' that, Gie fools their silks, and knaves their wine, A man's a man, for a' that.* She wondered if anyone dining below knew the words, or would care if they did.

She knew what she cared about. Or, more properly, who.

Alasdair sat beside her in the circle of chairs that Knox had arranged at the front of the drawing room, as far from the doors into the downstairs dining room as possible. He wore a neat bandage on his throat, and the open collar of his shirt was splattered now with rust-brown, not red. His expression wavering between elated and nauseated, Vasudev had offered dry-cleaning and medical specialists until Alasdair's polite smile grew pained. "If you'd have your chef prepare sandwiches . . ."

The platter of sandwiches sat empty on the end of the buffet. Funny how the risk of death sharpens the appetite, thought Jean, and tongued a bit of cress from between two back teeth. Today she and Alasdair were two for two.

For a' that an' a' that, It's coming yet for a' that, That man to man, the world o'er, Shall brithers be for a' that.

And what about sisters, Jean wondered. Knox had used both persuasion and threats to clear the entrance hall and the drawing room of reporters, allowing only Amy Herries to remain, under strict orders to keep her mouth shut. She sat at the far end of the buffet, just within earshot, her curly head bent over the handbag in her lap that she was apparently dismembering.

Knox and Gordon sat side by side, gazing across the circle of chairs at Des Bewley. Bewley was bookended by two large constables and handcuffed with garden-variety police-issue handcuffs, not the decorative variety from Pippa's across the lobby and up the stairs.

Through the drawing room doors, Jean saw Grizel fall once more from the landing, right before the oblivious faces of Ryan and another constable. Beside her, Alasdair tensed and then loosened again. She set her hand on his sleeve, sensing the subtle prickle of his force field.

Gordon held up a small plastic bag. Inside lay a blackened lump that could have been just about anything, but which Jean knew was a silver skull charm. "I was only finding it because I was told to be looking out for it. We likely'd never have gone looking for it without being tipped off there was something still at the scene. Even then, we were almost overlooking it in the shadows cast by the mortsafe, had to get the light of the torches shining just so."

A toddler could have guarded Bewley. He slumped, defeated. "Nicola wasn't half blazing I'd opened up the vault. How was I knowing 'twas the other end of the vault I'd bricked up, all these years ago?"

"You bricked up the vault?" Knox elbowed Gordon. He

tucked the bag into his coat and pulled out notebook and pen. Good, Jean thought. She didn't have to play steno—not that she had her notebook in her little evening bag anyway.

"Nicola, well, she was Chrissie then, just someone I was seeing at uni, all right? She liked a bit of the rough, I'm thinking, girl brought up proper in the Outer Isles and me from the banks of the Clyde, well accustomed to working. And to drinking."

There was something Nicola and Sara had in common, then. A strict upbringing. Funny, too, how a pendulum that had been pushed too far one way would come scything back too far to the other, given the chance.

"One night she came to me all in a panic," Bewley said. "Said she needed a doorway bricked up, there was something inside needed hiding. I'd been doing construction for a bit of the folding stuff, 'twasn't too hard getting the building supplies."

"Where was the door?" Gordon asked.

"At the back of the old Deacon's Neck Theater, behind the framing of an old fireplace. That building wasn't always a theater, used to be a hotel. Or a whorehouse, most likely. No surprise there'd be a hidey-hole. Chrissie—Nicola was saying she had a good friend doing a show there, she'd been hanging about and helping out, but something had gone terribly wrong and the friend was dead."

"That's all she told you?"

"Pretty near, aye."

"You've been blackmailing her all these years, have you?" asked Knox.

Bewley goggled at her. "Hell no. Why'd I be wanting to do that? Nicola, she looks after me is all. She's been throwing work my way. She fixed me up with the job at the Resurrectionist. I should've spit on Mr. Posh Prasad's shiny shoes and run like hell, that's what I should have done."

Alasdair fixed him with a stare like an icicle. "Rich, isn't it, your saying you were tired of all this happening on your doorstep, when you coshed the constable yourself. When you yourself tripped Jean here almost under the bus."

Jean very carefully did not let the memory of bus exhaust overcome the present aroma of food. "Because I was looking at the site of the theater? Because I was talking to Davis?"

Bewley stared at his hands, the metal cuffs holding them close together—but hardly in an attitude of prayer. "Davis. Not a clue, Davis. All that going on at the theater and he's seeing nowt but his own . . . Well."

"Why did you attack Ross?" Alasdair asked. "Asking questions about the crime scene, was he? Asking about Nicola?"

"She was telling me about the skull necklaces, way back when. Showing me hers—not that it was hers, she and her friend had traded. Then the friend ended up dead in the vault."

Amy stirred, stretched out the strap of her bag, knotted it again.

Knox asked, "And Nicola was thinking her skull charm was still there?"

"Aye."

"And you were after finding it for her?"

"She's always looking after me." The spittle sprayed from his lips. "Fifteen bloody years she's been looking after me. Wanted to show her that at the end of day, it's me could be saving her. But Ross, he was catching me going down there, went asking me why. After I looked after him as well. All that and I couldn't find the bleeding charm after all."

"You don't like clever people, do you?" Knox wasn't asking. To the constables she said, "Take him away. We'll be working up at least three charges of assault, perhaps even attempted murder. See if that will be making him feel himself a man again."

Gordon glanced over at her. "Feeling himself a man?"

She looked evenly back. "That's the problem, isn't it? That's always the problem."

"If you're saying so," Gordon replied, and flipped to a new page.

Hmmm, thought Jean. Beside her Alasdair watched the

constables drag Bewley away.

The front door opened and shut. Two more police people, one of them female, took up positions in the lobby. From downstairs wafted a pipe solo, making the dishes on the buffet jingle softly in accompaniment. Another constable—oh, Wallace, back in uniform—sat Ryan in the hot seat. The young man looked yearningly at the remains of the appetizers, then down at his empty hands. "You didn't put handcuffs on me."

"You're after attacking someone, are you?" Knox asked.

"Once was enough," he said. "Back then. Never again."

"I was arresting Bewley for assault, not murder. You, now . . ."

"I murdered Sara."

A quickly muffled moan came from Amy.

"Did you now?" asked Knox.

Ryan leaned forward, oozing desperation. "I met Sara at The Body Snatcher. She took me along to the theater. They could always use someone else with the scenery and stuff like that. She came on to me, really she did. All my hormones are in the right place—I'm not going to turn a pretty girl down."

Or even an ugly one, at that age, Jean thought.

"The janitor at the theater, an old guy who'd worked there forever, he'd disappear for hours at a time and come back drunk. Nobody ever saw him leave, though. Sara got him to show her where he went. Turned out he'd found a sliding panel in the frame of an old fireplace, one covering a doorway in a stone wall that had been thrown across the opening of a cave. It must have been in the steep ground leading down to the Cowgate. The muck in there, you wouldn't believe."

Knox opened her mouth, but Jean got there first. "What sort of muck? How had the place been used?"

"Petrified crap—cows and sheep, I think, but I'm no expert." Ryan's snort was only an imitation of a laugh. "Rotten clothes, rotten barrels, coils of metal tubing and stuff. Someone had a still in there, I bet, avoiding the revenuers."

"The excisemen, here," Jean said. When she had teased Miranda about the bricked-up doorway in Poe's "A Cask of

Amontillado", Miranda had come back with something about whisky distilling. The two of them should set up as stream-of-consciousness fortunetellers.

"What of the vault beneath the Playfair Building, where Sara's body was found?" asked Knox.

"And where Ranald Hamilton's body was found as well," Alasdair said.

"Who? Oh, the human bones. Yeah." Ryan leaned over, running his hands up over his face and through his hair as though they were a mask that he could pull off. "They were in a niche in the cave, wrapped up in some sort of decayed fabric. With the Bible and the cross. Sara moved them."

"Did she?" prompted Gordon.

"She and I went exploring and saw that the cave was tied into the vaults, but then we got to the dead end. Seriously, we had no clue it was just across the street from The Body Snatcher. From here. You get under the ground, you get disoriented."

Tell me about it, Jean thought. Alasdair set his hand on top of hers.

Ryan leaned over even further, drawing up his knees and resting his feet on the crossbar of the chair. "One night her friend Chrissie showed up. More than a friend, that was obvious. Sara was into experimentation, she'd try just about anything—drinking, mary jane, getting it on with another woman."

Knox asked, "Were you jealous, then?"

Amy dropped her bag to the floor and started knotting her hands instead.

"Some, maybe, but on the other hand, I was relieved she wanted to keep it all casual. Nicola, you're calling her now. Geez, does she look different. She's got real class. Then she was just a bitch, you know? Sticking her nose in here and there, trying to make points and get ahead."

"Make points with Davis?"

"Oh yeah. He gave her and Sara both those little skull charms, meant they were 'special'." His forefingers made quotation marks. "I bet he was having them shipped in from China by the boxcar load."

"And the two women fought," Alasdair said softly. "Over Davis?"

"Oh yeah. Over Davis. The three of us, Sara, Chrissie, me, we had a few drinks, we were having a good time—somewhere in the back of my mind I was hoping I could, you know, both the women at once . . ." He shrugged. "Anyway, Sara had us all go into the cave and move the bones into the vault and spread them out next to that old mortsafe. Don't know how that got in there, could have been the whisky guys collecting scrap metal—the poor people living in there had to scavenge anything they could, I guess, just trying to scratch a living."

True enough, Jean thought.

"Sara wanted to substitute the real mortsafe for this stupid one Davis had us make out of aluminum foil. She wanted to use some of the real bones in a scene where the ghost of Mary, Queen of Scots, wanders around looking for her head. A meeting of physical and social anthropology, Sara said. She must have gotten that from Davis. Man, could that guy run off at the mouth. Still can, I guess."

Jean offered no opinions. Gordon asked Ryan, "Did Davis know about this?"

"Not a clue. Not a hint of a clue. He didn't even know about the cave. Sara thought she'd make points by springing it all on him. He kept talking about pushing the envelope, and boy, that would have done it. The bones were just organic remains, she said, and Chrissie kept urging her on. Me, I kept telling her Davis wouldn't have the stomach for it. If she turned body snatcher herself she'd get him, all of us, in trouble with the authorities, and that would be the end of her being Miss Favorite."

"And would she be feeling that way about her own remains?" Knox asked, but not of anyone in particular.

Amy's intake of breath was almost a sob.

Cringing, Ryan folded in half like an animal protecting its soft underbelly. "I think I realized just about the time Sara did that Chrissie was egging her on because she wanted her to cause Davis trouble, she wanted her to lose status with him. Chrissie thought she'd be number one, then . . . That's where I've heard her called Nicola before. That's what she had Davis calling her. Already going for the posher name."

"And then?"

"Sara started calling Chrissie a traitor, saying she thought they were a couple, how could Chrissie stab her in the back like that. She was hurt, she was really hurt."

Gordon asked, "You're saying you were drunk as well, the three of you?"

"Yeah. That didn't help. When Sara dropped her flashlight and rushed at Chrissie, I tried to grab her, but I don't know exactly what happened . . ."

The music, the voices, the ring of silver against china seemed to fade. In the lobby, Grizel fell from the landing behind the backs of the waiting constables. Amy had apparently stopped breathing.

Ryan's voice trembled. "Somehow I threw her against the mortsafe. I don't know. It was dark. When I got the flashlights up and going again, there she was, one side of her, her head, all bloody, sort of crushed in—you could see, even in the dim light—she hit the corner of the mortsafe just right. Just wrong, that is. I murdered her."

Once again Jean remembered Ryan seizing her arm when she almost fell onto the mortsafe at Greyfriars. He'd gone white as a ghost, pale as one of Vasudev's tablecloths, ashen as the fires of an old passion.

The mortsafe in the vault wasn't rusty only with iron oxide, but with blood.

Alasdair's lips twitched. "You killed her, aye. You didn't murder her. Your account matches the forensics perfectly, the blood and hair on the corner of the mortsafe, the indentation in Sara's skull."

"Oh," Ryan said, the air rushing out of his chest as he realized he'd just passed the most important exam of his life.

At the far end of the buffet, Amy bent her face into her

hands and wept. Jean extricated her hand from Alasdair's, went to her, knelt at her side and wrapped her slender waist with her arm. In all the day's incidents, Alasdair hadn't told her about the forensics, that Knox already knew the identity of the—death weapon. Nothing would have changed if he had.

"And?" Knox asked Ryan.

"I ran away. I went home. I figured I'd have cops on my doorstep any minute, but no. Time passed and I realized Chrissie—Nicola—had covered it all up. I went on with my life. Then Jason said he was going to do a show in Edinburgh. And Vasudev Prasad called, said there was a ghost at his restaurant, and when he gave me the address I realized it was the old Body Snatcher. I wondered if it was Sara. I mean, we used to hang out there. I told Jason we needed to do a scene here as well as all the usual places, Greyfriars, the Castle. I wanted to know if it was her. If she was—happy."

Jean opened her mouth, then shut it again. Telling Ryan that the ghost wasn't Sara wouldn't help. If anything, it would shine a light into an area that didn't need illumination.

"Then Prasad ordered the vault beneath the Playfair Building opened up," said Gordon.

Ryan raised his reddened, tear-streaked face. "I saw it in the paper. I couldn't see how it could be the same vault, how the bodies could be Sara and the, the old one, until I walked around the area and put together the geography. Yes, it was her. Talk about being hoist with your own petard—they only opened the vault because we were in town . . ." He hiccupped. "I spent so much time walking around I got to Greyfriars late and tried to make lemonade out of lemons, you know, make points with Jason by giving him a bit extra to go on."

"Thanks," Amy said to Jean, and lurched to her feet. "I've heard enough. I'm away home. You're knowing where I am, eh, when it's coming to a trial? Any trial at all?"

Jean retrieved Amy's bag, levered herself to her own feet, and handed it over. Knox said, "We'll be in touch."

"Aye then, well . . ." Amy stopped beside Knox. "Thanks. And for being a strong woman as well. For setting an example.

I hope you do your sergeant here over properly, show him a man's not a man for all that, not in the way he's thinking, harassing you and all."

The female constable came forward and ushered Amy away.

Chapter Twenty-One

Knox stared after her. "What the hell?"

Gordon's mouth dropped open. "Where's she getting . . ."

Jean returned to her chair thinking, *Amy, I'm glad you're inspired by that harassment complaint but . . .*

Alasdair said under his breath, "Incoming."

Through the double doorway leading into the vaulted dining room walked Nicola, another female constable at her heels, one who shut the doors behind her just as Hugh and the lads struck up "Wild Mountain Thyme".

Nicola escorted herself to the hot seat and sat down. One solitary hair drooped from her upswept 'do. One micro-blot of lipstick marred the ivory of her front teeth. Other than that, she still looked as though she'd stepped from the pages of a fashion magazine.

She set her feet, in the black straps and spikes that constituted her shoes, side by side. Folding her hands in her lap, she stated, "Inspector Knox, I take full responsibility for the entire situation."

Jean wasn't the only one who'd been expecting a completely different statement. Alasdair's head went down as his brows went up. Gordon sat with his pen poised over a page. Knox actually emitted a dry cackle. "I beg your pardon, Miss MacLaren?"

"You're hearing me quite well. I'm the cause of it all. My decision first to help Sara with her mad scheme, then to conceal her accidental death, led all these years on to Des going about attacking folk. I'm sorry, Mr. Cameron. If I'd known he was taking matters into his own hands I'd have been jerking his choke-chain right smart."

"Anything," said Alasdair, "as long as you're by way of being in charge, is that it?"

Nicola didn't blink, but one corner of her red mouth tucked itself in affirmatively.

Knox ordered, "Let's be hearing the long and the short of it, then."

Nicola started at the beginning, taking them from Stornoway to Edinburgh University and the meeting with Sara Herries in one of Robin Davis's classes. "Most folk were still calling me Chrissie then, but I was wanting to be changing it, starting with Davis himself. Chrissie's a childish, girlish name, not the name of someone with connections. And a name implying an allegiance to an outdated system of religion and superstition."

"Did you find Davis," Jean asked, "or did he find you?"

"Both. Not that I was ever intending to throw over my practical studies in favor of his airy-fairy theories. But psychology and anthropology are part of marketing. I was seeing an advantage to forming an alliance with him. Besides," Nicola added, "he needed taking in hand. That revue of his, 'Ghosts for Fun and Profit', was beneath his dignity. *Commerce and Credibility* now, we're aiming that at a much more sophisticated audience."

"Do you have a sexual relationship with him?" asked Knox.

Nicola laughed. "Oh, please. Hardly."

"What of your relationship with Sara?"

"She was playing about. Although, given the chance and another choice of fathers, she might have eventually come out of the closet. Then—well, I was telling her never to mind with Allsort, but she was thinking she needed a boyfriend, to be covering for the girlfriend. He was doing her no good, was Allsort. Tristan Ryan, I'm hearing now. He went telling what happened that night in the vault, did he?"

"It's time you were telling us what happened," said Knox.

"Sara was after using the real bones in Davis's juvenile revue. Big mistake, I was telling her. There's a saying, there's no such thing as bad publicity, but at the university, there is."

Tell me about it, Jean thought, and caught Alasdair's sidelong glance.

Knox cocked her head to the side, but apparently decided whether or not Nicola had been urging Sara on was a secondary issue right now.

"We'd been drinking. Another mistake, I'm realizing that now. We had a row. She came for me. I pushed her away just as Allsort went grabbing at her and . . ." Nicola's eyes looked beyond the room, beyond the night, into the past. "She fell against the corner of the mortsafe."

Gordon stated, "She died."

"We tried CPR. No good. Out like a light. Gone."

Jean remembered the lights going out in the vault, closed her eyes, and opened them again on the brightly lit, classically decorated room.

"We tried CPR," Nicola repeated. "We broke her necklace and the skull went flying. My skull. We'd traded, hers for mine, sisters, she was saying. Lovers." Again her eyes went distant.

"You covered up her death," said Knox, "hoping to save what you were expecting to be a brilliant career."

Nicola nodded. The shiny red fingernails of her right hand dug into the palm of her left, leaving red crescents in the fair skin. "Then there was Des Bewley, my version of Allsort in a way, but a nastier piece of work, a bit of a yob, something I was foolish enough to find exciting. Like Davis, I was taking him in hand, if in a different sort of way. I had him brick up the door to the cave. I left Sara lying there in the dark."

After a moment of silence, Jean said, "Bewley was a reclamation project. You wanted to reform him." And she had once thought Alasdair was a reclamation project.

"I've failed at that, haven't I? Who's been helping whom? Who's been using whom?"

"Was it Bewley who told you P.C. Ross's name?" Alasdair asked.

"Yes. Does it matter?"

Knox answered. "Ross told us he saw you ticking Bewley off. For unblocking the door in the cellar of the Playfair Building?"

"I was afraid it led into the same vault where Sara—where Sara's been all these years. I was right. I knew the skull with my initials was still lying there. I was right about that. It was my original decision that's gone so badly wrong." Having circled back to where she came in, Nicola sat up straight, laid her hand flat on her black-clad knees, and looked Knox in the eye. "Are you planning on charging me, Inspector? With what? Covering up a death? Surely there's a statute of limitations."

"Let's get you to the office for a formal statement," Knox replied. "Then we'll be discussing possible charges."

"All right. I've left instructions, the rest of the dinner should be getting on without my supervising." But her glance over her shoulder at the doors to the dining room belied her words. Surely no one could put food on their plates without her oversight.

"Come along then." Gordon stood up and the two constables stepped forward.

Nicola rose onto her shoes, perfectly balanced. She looked over at Jean and Alasdair. "Any time you're feeling like shopping at Pippa's, Miss Fairbairn, I'd be happy to arrange a discount. Good night."

Gordon offered Jean and Alasdair both a quick salute, retrieved Nicola's coat, and disappeared into the lobby. As the front door shut, Grizel fell from the staircase. Yes, there had been a lot of emotion spilled here tonight. No wonder the ghost was restless. Not happy, in Ryan's words.

Alasdair and Jean managed to lever each other up out of their chairs. Oh good, her blood was circulating. Alasdair's kilt was swinging. If all wasn't right with the world, at least it was all right enough to be going on with.

Alasdair said to Knox, "Ryan's by way of being a wild card, Bewley's a loose cannon, and Nicola, well, you might not be finding anything to go charging her with."

"Not for lack of trying," replied Knox.

"It's not fair," Jean said, "that Davis is getting off scot-free—sorry—but then, so did Burke and Hare's Dr. Knox. Although he was a lot more culpable. He knew what was going on."

"My ancestor might have known what was going on . . ." Knox raised her hand. *Don't go there.* ". . . but I'm not so sure Robin Davis did do. No matter. He'll be having a few conversations with me before we're quite finished. Me, I'm thinking he deserves Nicola."

Jean nodded. "I'm thinking that, too."

Alasdair rotated his shoulders. The bandage on his neck pulled, and he winced. "Ironic, that the cave likely was coming within inches of being discovered during the clean-up from the 2002 fire. And the other end of the tunnel as well, during the renovations here at Lady Niddry's."

"A shame it wasn't," Knox said, turning toward the door. "Might have been someone else's case. If you'll be excusing me then, I'm away. Thank you for your assistance, Mr. Cameron. If you'd not forced the issue, I'm not sure we'd have worked all this out."

"Jean forced the issue," Alasdair told her. "But you're welcome, in any event."

Jean felt her tongue loosening, never mind she'd had almost nothing to drink. "Just one more thing, Inspector Knox. What's up with you and Gordon, anyway? Amy heard someone say something about a sexual harassment complaint."

Knox stopped. Her back stiffened. She couldn't see Alasdair covering his face with his hand and shaking his head. *Jean, for the love of . . .*

She blundered on. "As if I hadn't already had way too many lessons on setting priorities and so forth. I got two more today. We got two more today. Don't let the situation go unresolved. Demand an apology. Transfer him somewhere else. Go ahead and file the complaint."

Knox spun completely around, her eyes bulging in what Jean hoped was astonishment rather than resentment. Her voice was crisp as a winter day. "There's talk of a complaint, yes. Against me. I made him an offer, suggested a colleagues-with-benefits arrangement. He refused. Said he wasn't mingling work with recreation."

Mentally Jean hit her forehead with her palm. *Duhhh* . . . "Okay. Yeah. Amy jumped to conclusions. So did I. That's my favorite sport, jumping to conclusions."

In her peripheral vision, she saw Alasdair emerge from behind his hand, features set soberly but a suspicious twitch gathering at the corners of his mouth.

She saw Gordon step into the lobby door, brows approaching his hairline.

Knox, now, Knox hadn't yet blinked.

In for a lamb, Jean told herself, in for a sheep. "Has it occurred to you that he's threatening to file a complaint not because of your, ah, offer, but because of the way you've been acting over his refusal? Picking on him? Either way, you're letting personal issues interfere with your work."

Knox's lashes rose and fell. Her lips thinned and loosened.

"Take my advice, Wendy," Jean concluded. "Get over yourself and deal with it. Letting something like this fester, it's not worth it."

Knox's astonishment cracked into rueful laughter. She gazed down at Jean as though wanting to pat her on the head. Instead she said, "If the man's wanting a transfer, he's got it. If the man's filing a complaint, so be it. He's a fine sergeant, but I've driven him away, haven't I?"

From the doorway Gordon said, "That's all depending, isn't it now?"

Knox spun around. They exchanged a long look that passed so far above Jean's head they might as well have been signals between transmission towers.

Knox said over her shoulder, "There are times you seize the day, there are times you let it go, eh? Time you were letting this one go, Jean. Good night." She marched through the lobby, Gordon at her side, past Grizel falling from the staircase and out into the night.

Jean felt the last burst of energy draining from her limbs. "Sorry."

But Alasdair was grinning. "Some things need saying. Some things need doing." He started off toward the staircase, moving as slowly as if through deep water. Deep cold water.

Placing one foot in front of the other, she followed Alasdair across the icy black-and-white tiles, beneath the glow of the chandelier. He jockeyed first right, then left beneath the landing.

There she was, on the brink, hands folded in prayer. Eyes downcast in certainty.

She fell.

With a grunt of effort, Alasdair caught her.

For one split second, the ephemeral shape nestled in the living arms, soft gray-white against tartan. For one split second Grizel's eyes saw eternity, and the peace that passed all understanding.

Then she was gone, into air that thinned instantly from viscous cold to cool and scented with food. She—it—was no more than memory, one of the many memories thronging this ancient city.

Alasdair straightened. After a long, silent moment he turned to Jean. "Right."

"Right," she replied. "So if the anonymous waiter with the ghost allergy ever comes back, will he wonder where she went? Or will he be relieved she's gone on to wherever she wanted to go . . ." Jean's voice died away. From downstairs came Hugh's mellow tenor singing, "Caledonia's been everything I've ever had."

She took Alasdair's arm. He pressed his cheek into the top of her head. "I've never asked how you enjoyed your visit to Pippa's, up the stairs. Expanded your horizons, did it?"

"No. There's really no place like home."

"Then it's time that's where we were going."

Close together, side by side, they turned toward the door, and didn't look back.

For a map of the area of Edinburgh where the story takes place and a diagram of the South Bridge vaults, please see Lillian's website: www.lillianstewartcarl.com/b.mortsafe.

The Mortsafe is half the length of the first five books in the series.

About the Author

After starting out in science fiction and fantasy, Lillian Stewart Carl is now writing contemporary novels blending mystery, romance, and fantasy, along with short mystery and fantasy stories. Her work often includes paranormal themes. It always features plots based on history and archaeology. While she doesn't write comedy, she believes in characters with a sense of humor. Her novels have been compared to those of Daphne du Maurier, Mary Renault, Mary Stewart (no relation), Barbara Michaels/Elizabeth Peters, and J.R.R. Tolkien's colleague Charles Williams.

Her fantasies are set in a mythological, alternate-history Mediterranean and India. Her contemporary novels are set in Texas, in Ohio, in Colonial Williamsburg, Virginia, and in England and Scotland.

Of *Shadows in Scarlet,* Publishers Weekly says, "Presenting a delicious mix of romance and supernatural suspense, Carl (*Ashes to Ashes*) delivers yet another immensely readable tale. She has created an engaging cast and a very entertaining plot, spicing the mix with some interesting twists on the ghostly romantic suspense novel."

Of *Lucifer's Crown, Library Journal* says: "Blending historical mystery with a touch of the supernatural, the author creates an intriguing exploration of faith and redemption in a world that is at once both modern and timeless."

Among many other novels, Lillian is the author of the Jean Fairbairn/Alasdair Cameron cross-genre mystery series: America's exile and Scotland's finest on the trail of all-too-living legends. Of *The Secret Portrait*, *Kirkus* says: "Mystery, history and sexual tension blend with a taste of the wild beauty of the Highlands." Of *The Burning Glass*, *Publishers Weekly* says: "Authentic dialect, detailed descriptions of the castle and environs, and vivid characters recreate an area rich in history and legend. The tightly woven plot is certain to delight history fans with its dramatic collision of past and present."

With John Helfers, Lillian co-edited *The Vorkosigan Companion*, a retrospective on Lois McMaster Bujold's science fiction work, which was nominated for a Hugo award.

Her first story collection, *Along the Rim of Time*, was published in 2000, and her second, *The Muse and Other Stories of History, Mystery, and Myth*, in 2008, including three stories that were reprinted in *Year's Best* mystery anthologies.

Her books are available in both print and electronic editions. Her website is www.lillianstewartcarl.com, and she has a fan page on Facebook.

Made in the USA
San Bernardino, CA
25 May 2014